SIMON OKOTIE was born to a Nigerian father and an English mother. He lives in London. This is his first novel.

WHATEVER HAPPENED TO HAROLD ABSALON?

SIMON OKOTIE

CROMER

PUBLISHED BY SALT PUBLISHING
12 Norwich Road, Cromer NR27 0AX United Kingdom

First published by Salt Publishing, 2012

Printed in Great Britain by Clays Ltd, St Ives plc

Typeset in Paperback 9.5/14.5

ISBN 978 1 907773 34 1 paperback

1 3 5 7 9 8 6 4 2

For Maitreyabandhu

1

The hotel lobby was both cleansed and fragrant, as was the receptionist speaking softly on the phone behind the desk. The owners obviously wanted to welcome people to their establishment, to encourage them to return there for further visits or to recommend it to their friends and associates. The owners wanted this to take place so they could make money – that was the primary reason, Marguerite thought. Personally, he had insufficient funds to stay at that or any other hotel – it was not just an issue of people wanting beds and the hotel providing them, along with other facilities, perhaps, such as a restaurant. You really did need money or a means of payment to cover your temporary residence there. It might not be your own money: you might be there to attend a conference, for instance, if you were a white-collar worker, in which case your employers may have paid for your stay at the hotel. As a blue-collar worker you might be visiting a nearby factory, say, from your home in another part of the world, and you might need to stay overnight at the hotel. In this latter instance, there would be a judgement by your boss (who would almost always be a white-collar worker – who would work, that is, in the office as well as occasionally, perhaps, on the factory floor) about whether or not you would be able to get back from your visit in the same day and/or whether it would be so inconvenient for you to do so that it would be worth staying over, as it is known. Your boss would judge whether, for instance, you would get home after midnight, which is to say in the early hours, rather than at your normal seven or eight o'clock, back for your evening meal, perhaps prepared by your wife, always, in fact, to Marguerite's mind, prepared by your wife, who would not have a job of her own, who could not be categorised into white- or blue-collar, who would always simply be there. In the case where you stayed over, she would receive a phone call from you, perhaps from the office of the firm you were visiting, just as you were leaving there to go to the hotel, or perhaps from the hotel itself just after you had arrived there, once you had checked in, to say that you had arrived, that you had checked in, if you had, that the visit to the other firm went well, or went badly, or went some other way in between those two options or outside of them, such as 'it went very well' or 'it went exceptionally well' or 'it went really badly', and it would be a novelty to make that call, especially from the hotel, to say that you were making that call from the hotel or from the B&B.

And there would be nothing to stop you, with the blessing of your white-collar boss, from taking your wife with you. Your boss would perhaps justify this in his mind by the fact that you, a valued and trusted employee, were doing a job for him, a white-collar job that is, for a couple of days that he might have had to do himself, and that you

2

were going out of your way to do it, as it were, spending more time than you would ordinarily be contracted to do, and it would not cost the firm (your firm) any more money probably for your wife to go on the trip with you, 'to keep you company' – your boss would perhaps put it in those terms – on the long journey because, as has already been established, implicitly if not explicitly, it would need to be a long journey otherwise your boss would not have approved your stay at the hotel, perhaps giving you some 'petty cash' to cover other expenses along the way, such as petrol or food. There would be no harm, then, in you taking your wife along with you on the trip – many hotels will give you a double room even if you are a single person. That is to say that many (at least) hotel beds (that is, beds in hotels) are double (at least) in size and some (no doubt) are queen- or king-size (a size that will be defined in due course) and the marginal costs associated with staying in such a room as a single person compared to a couple were not as great as the difference between a single person staying or not staying at that hotel.

The blue-collar worker in question would, Marguerite thought, be quite senior in the firm or would, at least, be quite senior amongst the ranks of the blue-collar workers at the firm, even perhaps being the most senior – in terms of age or years of service at that firm or total years of service – or would be the most trustworthy and/or responsible individual in those ranks, and would thus be justified in taking, with the blessing of his boss, or the firm's owner, or both, or both in one (that is if the owner also runs the firm day-to-day), his (that is, the blue-collar worker's) wife with him on the visit to the other firm, that visit involving a journey of some distance from his home or from his own firm, thereby necessitating a stay in a hotel which, for convenience (and common sense) reasons would be a much shorter distance from the firm that he was visiting than his (and his wife's) own home was. The boss or owner or both or both-in-one would make the judgement that they were prepared to fund the marginal costs of the couple compared to the single person to compensate their senior blue-collar worker for the additional time spent in making the visit to the other firm. It would be seen by the senior blue-collar worker in question and his wife as a perk of his position as one of, or the, senior blue-collar worker in the firm, which is to say one of the senior blue-collar worker*s*, or *the* senior blue collar worker, or the most experienced (in that firm or in other firms) or the most trustworthy and/ or responsible of that rank of worker at that firm or one of the workers seen in those terms by the management and owners of that firm or both or both-in-one.

It was much more routine for the white-collar worker to stay in a hotel. That is not to say that the above considerations did not enter the mind of the white-collar worker or his boss (etc). It is just to say that it is unlikely that there would be the same frisson of excitement in the white-collar worker's mind that existed in the blue-collar worker's mind under the scenario described. The other consideration in this distinction between blue- and white-collar workers and their respective visits to an hotel (and notice that the use of 'an', in this instance, itself adds a frisson of perhaps sexual excitement to the word hotel and that the means by which it does this is by effectively silencing the 'h', thereby transporting, at a stroke, the hotel from the Anglo Saxon world to the Gallic world, with the concomitant sense of style and relaxed sexual expressiveness that that entails) was that the white-collar worker would be more likely, in Marguerite's mind, to be female rather than male, in which case one would have to reverse the example from wife-companion to husband-companion. This brought up any number of issues of masculinity, 'bread-winning' and male potency for the husband-companion that Marguerite did not have the urge or the inclination to go into, at least not at that moment.

The other advantage of the wife accompanying (in the case of the blue- or white-collar worker) or the husband accompanying (in the case of the white-collar worker and, Marguerite conceded, very occasionally or occasionally, in the case of the blue-collar worker) their spouse on the trip and for the stay in the hotel was that it dispelled, or at least reduced, any suspicion that the husband or wife undertaking the trip (that is, the prime mover) was having an affair and that the trip itself was just a cover for that affair. It did not completely dispel the suspicion that the blue- or white-collar worker may be having an affair of course. The request to the husband or wife to accompany their spouse could indeed be part of the web of deception and calculation designed to send the spouse off the scent for a little while longer in relation to the affair that the husband or wife was engaged in. The reader will no doubt be familiar, from other forms, with the exposure of the call to the manager (etc) of the firm who asks the innocent (to their mind) question 'What trip?', and with that simple question lays bare the web of deception and calculation that the husband or wife had been engaged in for perhaps some time, as had been the case with Isobel Absalon just before her husband disappeared. Now, in following Isobel Absalon into the hotel and seeing her disappear, with a pushchair, into the lift, Marguerite wanted simply to find out whether – and if so, how – the hotel that he had just entered related to Harold Absalon's disappearance, whilst I, in turn, want to know what will happen to me when he's found[a].

Knowing that he could only continue his surveillance whilst the receptionist remained on the telephone and was therefore unable to apprehend him, Marguerite focused again on the numbers above the lift doors and noticed that Isobel Absalon had reached the second storey of the hotel.

a. They started calling me 'Harold' in the project office shortly after he disappeared. I thought it was a joke to start with, and ignored it. But I just couldn't shake it off.

2

The bed involved in Harold Absalon's case was king- rather
than queen-sized, the latter being smaller than the former,
even though some queens, surely, were larger than some
kings. Was it an average that was taken? It seemed more
likely to Marguerite that the sizes were modelled on particular monarchs – perhaps on a regal couple where the
king (say, Henry VIII) was more sizeable than the queen(s),
in which case what happened in other countries? If it were
one particular king and queen, whether they were a couple
or otherwise, upon whom the sizes were modelled then was
it only in the motherland and in the former colonies[b] that
such sizes existed? Was it, in fact, one of these former colonies that had coined the terms king- and queen-sized with
due deference to the monarch who had been presiding at
that time? But what if the terms were coined at different
times, as now seemed more likely to Marguerite? Surely
king-sized beds appeared first, with queen-sized beds

b. Harold Absalon was from a different background to the others in the
office but was, at the same time, their superior. That was what I found so
interesting about him when he first arrived. So often, in that situation, when
someone was from a different background to the great mass of the people
then they would not, or could not, be led by that person. No, when someone
was different and found themselves in that position of authority then there
could be real problems – people would want, in my experience, to tear that
person apart.

appearing perhaps much later. In that case he thought it unlikely that the king and queen in question were a couple, that they had reigned in concord, so to speak, had sat on the throne at the same time, had sat on their thrones at the same time, during, that is, their shared reign, rather than at the same time of day, when they were not in their bed. And this brought to mind another matter which strengthened Marguerite's conviction that the king and queen in question did not reign concurrently, which was this: what size of bed would they have slept in had they reigned together, that is if they had shared a bed? The Queen in this instance might object to sleeping (or simply being, at those moments when she wasn't sleeping) in a bed the proportions of which suited her husband much better; she might feel somewhat lost in its expanses, assuming that this is a case in which the queen was smaller in height, but not necessarily in girth, than the king. Similarly the king might object (with more reason, to Marguerite's mind) to having to deal with the dimensions of a queen-sized bed – Marguerite pictured the regal male feet hanging beyond the edge of plushness, and the king perhaps getting a chill, which could, if it developed into pneumonia, precipitate any number of constitutional crises, assuming that the king, again, were taller than the queen in this example.

In fact, Marguerite remembered, as he watched the number three light up above the lift doors, that the sizes 'king-' and 'queen-' referred, in fact, to the width, rather than the length, of the bed. All of his reflections relating to height rather than girth should, then, be disregarded. Instead the wing span of the monarch should be considered, with the bejewelled royal hands hanging over the side replacing the royal toes at the end of the bed in discomforted chill. Notice that the two regal size categories conveyed nothing about the *style* of bed. Marguerite's view was that one typically imagines kings and queens alike sleeping in four-poster beds, the overhead structure of which must, therefore, reflect the size (king- or queen-) of the bed itself. The size says nothing about the curtains and other drapes flowing down the sides of the king's and/or queen's bed so that it almost forms a room in itself, one in which the servants do not have access, or only in the most exceptional circumstances, which have not been adequately documented in the history books to Marguerite's mind. The absence of any such drapery in Harold Absalon's case – or, indeed, of any overhead structure whatsoever – had afforded surveillance a clear sight of the scene. It was this footage that had set Marguerite on the trail of Isobel Absalon, the wife of the missing transport advisor, whom, he noticed, had just passed through the fourth floor of the hotel.

3

The receptionist continued speaking on the telephone at the desk behind him, but he could only make out the odd word of what she was saying. She was not talking continuously. If she had been talking continuously it would have meant that the person on the other end of the line would not have been getting a word in, as it is known. It was no doubt for this reason that the receptionist was speaking intermittently, in response, perhaps, to questions being put to her by the person on the other end of the line or, alternatively, as a means of asking her own questions. Her mainly asking or answering questions would depend in large part, Marguerite thought, on whether the caller was booking a room in the hotel, in which case the receptionist would be asking most of the questions – length of stay, single, twin or double room, en suite facilities, king- or queen-sized bed, etc – or was merely enquiring about staying in the hotel, in which case the caller would be asking most of the questions, perhaps, and the receptionist would mainly be answering, and answering in a persuasive, encouraging and helpful manner if she wanted the person to stay at the hotel or in a less persuasive, encouraging and helpful manner if she couldn't care less whether they stayed at the hotel. Either way, Marguerite knew that the receptionist would effectively be tied to the desk for the duration of the call, and for as long as that situation pertained she would not be able to apprehend him.

Marguerite would only take the lift if the receptionist remained on the phone once the lift had returned to ground. Were the receptionist to have finished on the phone before the lift returned to ground, then Marguerite would take the stairs since, in this latter scenario, he risked being apprehended by the receptionist if he continued waiting for the lift. What prevented him from taking the stairs straight away? Taking the stairs would have meant that he would have been unable to observe which floor Isobel Absalon had travelled to. Given that he wanted to observe this, he continued to wait in front of the lift, glancing at the numerals as they illuminated in turn, the receptionist continuing to murmur behind and to one side of him.

But he also risked something in his waiting to decide whether to take the lift or the stairs: if he was going to use the end of the receptionist's telephone conversation as the starting point for running up the stairs, then he would need to concentrate more intently on the sounds coming from the reception desk – he needed to be able to hear the sound of the receiver being replaced in the cradle (if that is what it was called) of the phone, perhaps with a click, and then *that* would be his pistol shot and he would be off. But it would be a very quiet start, and it might allow the receptionist to have a head start on him, a head start which, high heels or no high heels, could prove crucial in her apprehending him. And those high heels could easily (presumably) be flicked off under the desk towards the end of the call, assuming that they were high heels and that they had not already been flicked off under the desk for comfort, say, or through force of habit, meaning that she would also have that relative advantage, namely stockinged feet compared to high heels in or on which to pursue him.

Partly it would depend on how the receptionist ended the call. Some people (especially some women) ended calls with 'Yes . . . thank you . . . thank you . . . OK, thank you . . . sure . . . sure . . . OK . . . yes . . . thanks . . . bye . . . bye . . . bye . . . ', which was a countdown to a starting pistol if ever he'd heard one, a 'Take your marks . . . set . . .' (but in different language). Others were more abrupt in their partings, especially, perhaps, in the more professional environment that he assumed himself to be in, whether they were men or women. But who was to say that the call was a professional call relating to the smooth running of the hotel, or whether the receptionist had received a personal call on this occasion?

The call was continuing, the number five had just lit up above the lift doors and Marguerite appeared to have plenty of time to really explore what it meant for his investigations that Isobel Absalon, the wife of the missing transport advisor, continued to move up the lift shaft of that hotel in that particular part of that particular city.

4

Marguerite reached out and pressed the button beside the lift door. One could tell so much from the presence of this button, he reflected, whilst listening for movement from the desk behind him. What this button conveyed to Marguerite, at least, was that there was only one direction that the lift could travel in: upwards. He did not know if there were lifts that travelled in other directions (aside, of course, from downwards): left, right, or any of the other (would they be called cardinal?) directions in between. By some fortuitous combination of factors, including the effects of gravity (or, possibly, primarily due to the effects of gravity), there was no need to even look into the possibility that Isobel Absalon had travelled diagonally up or down the building. There was a lift *shaft* and, crudely, a series of pulleys that dragged the moveable room up and down that shaft. The situation would have been very strange indeed for it to have been otherwise; he couldn't rule it out completely, however: Harold Absalon might have been a spy – he had, after all, worked in government, albeit local government; Marguerite knew that the era of the Soviets had long passed, but he also knew that spies still existed and that, by their very nature, one didn't know who was a spy and who wasn't (on the whole). This could have been an intelligence HQ, then, as it would probably be called, just masquerading as a hotel – he couldn't rule it out completely. If that were the case then any number of almost unimaginable things could have happened to the lift once the doors had closed on Isobel Absalon that after-noon. And that was why he must just hold his nerve, as it is known, keep tailing her and continue his investigation, even though he could sense the receptionist's telephone conversation slowly coming to a close and what he took to be the crackle of what's known as a walkie-talkie behind and to one side of him.

But how could he be sure that Isobel Absalon was still in the lift, he now wondered? He judged that the lift had not stopped by the fact that each subsequent number contin-ued to light up for about the same amount of time as the preceding one and that this amount of time was not incon-sistent with the amount of time he had observed other lift lights to be illuminated when the lift was still ascend-ing rather than being more or less stationary. He had, in short, been in lifts before and had noted the duration of each numeral's illumination when the lift was travelling upwards or downwards. He hadn't realised it until that moment, but he had internalised this study so that, now that he was watching the lights above the outer lift door on the ground floor of the hotel, he could judge that the lift had not stopped in its ascent of the building, even though each illuminated number stayed illuminated for a period before moving on to the next.

But what if Isobel Absalon had entered the lift and

immediately exited it, Marguerite wondered, as he watched the lift indicator move through seven? He had watched her enter the lift with her pushchair as he was entering the hotel and could not tell whether there had been another set of doors on the rear wall of the lift. He could not, therefore, conclusively rule out the possibility that she had entered the lift and immediately exited it, ie had remained on the ground floor without ascending the floors as indicated above the front outer door of the lift.

On reflection, the combination of two points in particular made it unlikely, if not impossible, that Isobel Absalon would have entered and immediately exited the lift on the ground floor. The first point was that there had been insufficient time for Isobel Absalon to have exited before the lift had started to ascend. The reason that Marguerite judged there to have been insufficient time was that he had entered the hotel just as Isobel Absalon was entering the lift with the pushchair. He had managed to get to the lift doors just as they were closing. He thought it unlikely that Isobel Absalon would enter and immediately exit the lift, ie before the doors had fully closed, thereby blowing her cover, as it is known, and, given he'd heard the lift moving immediately after the doors had closed, he judged it unlikely that she had immediately exited the lift in the way described. Besides, he had been monitoring the situation from the start with the aid of the numerical indicator, and the 'G' had not remained illuminated for long enough to enable Isobel Absalon to effect an immediate exit, assuming for the time being that the indicator was reliable. Secondly, Marguerite thought it unlikely, now, that

Isobel *or* Harold Absalon (or both) worked for the secret services and that this was an intelligence HQ of some sort where the numbers above the lift doors did not correspond (give or take – never precisely, of course) with the motion (upwards or downwards) of the lift or with those moments when the lift was stationary; or where the lift, or its occupants, could travel in a diagonal, traverse or (what were the other options? – he would look into them) other direction when the numbers simply continued to ascend in a reasonably orderly fashion. He thought it even more unlikely that Isobel Absalon had unwittingly stumbled into an intelligence HQ masquerading as a hotel, where the illuminated floor indicator did not tally with the lift itself, or where the lift itself could travel in all sorts of directions, ie not just up and down. He therefore concluded that Isobel Absalon was very, very likely still to be in the lift and that she was still moving counter-gravitationally with the lift through that core of the building that was called the lift shaft.

5

Glancing at the floor numbers above the lift doors, Marguerite was shocked to see that he had missed the number at which Isobel Absalon had disembarked. The number illuminated was consistently lower now than the previously illuminated number, whereas previously it had been consistently higher. She must have disembarked, he thought; at least she was very likely to have done so, given the fact that the lift was now descending. How could an agent of his calibre have slipped up in this way, he wondered? Had he become distracted by the soft voice and scent of the receptionist at the desk behind him? It couldn't be ruled out. Fortunately, he was able to reapply his fine mind to the problem and he came to the following satisfying and surprisingly rapid conclusion. The last time he had noticed the lift indicator it had been at floor seven. It had gone past floor seven – he had also noticed that. He had not noticed at that time that the top floor was floor eight – that was where the numbers ended, at least. He concluded that that was where Isobel Absalon had alighted from the lift. Unsure that the receptionist would remain on the telephone until the lift had returned to the ground floor, he moved past the lift and through the door to the stairwell.

As he started up the stairs, he wondered why stair lifts did not have floor indicators. Was it because they would only generally traverse one flight of stairs (and notice here that this particular lift *does* move diagonally, and that such lifts were not generally located in some secret service establishment, but were lifts that mainly old people would have in their homes and care homes, lifts which were used when the primary mode of transportation – walking, with the legs as the primary or (for most) the sole means of loco-motion – had stopped functioning sufficiently well to carry them upstairs)? If it was because they generally only tra-versed one flight of stairs then it (ie the lack of a lift indica-tor) could be to do with the fact that when the legs gave out and wouldn't propel one upstairs any longer – as was the case, he thought, with most users of stair lifts – then one would typically have some sort of attendant to look over one, especially when one was undertaking certain manoeu-vres such as going upstairs. One would generally have an attendant, he thought, who would know where one was, who would stand at the bottom of the flight of stairs or on the landing, as it was called, and simply watch one ascend or descend. So there would be no need for an indicator in this instance. One person would know where one was at any time.

He had used the word attendant quite loosely, but it would serve his purpose, he thought. The attendant could, for instance, be the old person's wife (if he were a man) or husband (if she were a woman) (and notice the shift in the third-person pronoun as the examples shift gender); the wife, or husband, would be very likely to be old folks themselves; this would mean that they would be more likely, in Marguerite's view, to use the stair lift themselves, when it was finished with; in that case they would attend to their husband (or wife) as they ascended (or descended) (and there is no correlation between male spouse and ascension and female spouse and descension) and then would be attended to in turn by husband or wife as they themselves used the lift to ascend or descend. It is clear, in this case, that no indicator is required – they would simply be able to see the lift itself ascending or descending provided their eyesight was good enough, just as in the case of a glass lift (which implies also a glass lift shaft or a glass façade to the lift shaft).

If someone were trying to find a relation, say, in this case then they could either: a) look at the stair lift itself to see if it contained the person they were looking for (their husband or wife, mother or father, grandfather or grandmother would be the main dyads); or, b) if they couldn't see the person in the stair lift, perhaps because it had gone around a corner, they could ask the attendant where the person they were looking for was located. In the case where the attendant was the spouse of the person in the stair lift, not only would they ask where the person they were looking for was located but they may also exchange a few pleasantries, as they are known, with the so-called attendant, or more pleasantries (quantity, not quality) than if they were a mere attendant (and Marguerite did have the utmost respect for the 'mere' attendant – he didn't want to denigrate them in any way). They would exchange pleasantries for longer (shall we say) in the former case than in the latter, ie the case where the attendant were the spouse of the person in the stair lift (and the words chair lift also entered Marguerite's consciousness now, with the glistening white plains of snow fields, and he remembered that Isobel and Harold Absalon had been on a skiing holiday together before their child was born, a holiday that hadn't gone altogether smoothly, shall we say). This would be because they would be related to that person, and it is a law of nature that we take more interest in the well being of our blood relations than we do of others[c]. It is a law of nature, but that doesn't mean that it is always true. Never mind that for now.

Marguerite could hear knives and forks on plates, and spoons on bowls, as soon as he rather breathlessly opened the door at the top of the stairwell, that is, on the eighth floor. He realised with contentment that there was a more or less direct correlation between spoon and bowl, at least between dessert/soup spoon and bowl, and teaspoon and cup/mug, or sometimes (in the case of a latte in a tall glass with a handle) glass. He took delight in this correspondence. The reason for it was simple enough – bowls and cups generally contained foodstuffs that tended more to liquid than to solid form and the spoon was the item of cutlery par excellence for transferring such foodstuffs between receptacle and mouth. The fork could be used for the dessert – there was no denying that. All he was assert-

c. It was, perhaps, an issue of trust. If your background was so different, how could others know that you shared the same, or similar, values? How could you know that your thinking overlapped, as it were, with theirs? So that was what struck me about him, that he could lord it over the others, even though they were not of his kith and kin. I admired him for it. And I immediately wanted what he wanted.

ing in this particular analytical flourish was that the spoon and the bowl (or, more specifically, the dessert spoon and the dessert bowl, or the soup spoon and the soup bowl, or the teaspoon and tea/coffee cup) went together, were natural partners; it was another argument altogether to say that the dessert spoon always went with dessert, or that the knife and fork always went with the main course. Only a rhetorician of the very lowest orders would bring forward such a proposition.

On moving through the doorway, an attendant of a very different kind to that cited in the stair lift situation immediately approached him. 'And what can we do for you, my friend?' he asked sarcastically. Marguerite simply smiled and looked past him at the tables of diners in the bright restaurant. He spotted Isobel Absalon sitting with a female friend at one of the tables, the pushchair, which contained a very young child, to one side of them. The friend, in fact, had her arm around Isobel Absalon, who was smiling painfully. Satisfied, for now, with this observation, Marguerite allowed himself to be escorted by the attendant towards the lift, knowing that he could continue his surveillance of Isobel Absalon, her friend, and what he took to be Isobel and Harold Absalon's child, from outside the hotel.

6

Marguerite found himself on his hands and knees on the pavement just outside the lobby. Getting to his feet, as it is known, he realised that he needed to look around the hotel to check whether there were any other means of entry or escape. In other words, he needed to 'case the joint'; he had heard this term during his training and thought it appropriate here. What he wanted to ensure was that there was no way that Isobel Absalon could exit the hotel without him knowing. The reason he didn't want her to exit the hotel without him knowing was because he thought that she would inexorably (or not, thereby covering all eventualities) lead him to Harold Absalon – how could she not? It was too hot a trail to turn down, in other words. He would, then, have to ensure that, given that this hotel was not a secret service establishment of some sort, or even an HQ, there was no other way for her to escape his pursuit. He would look for other routes out of the building to ensure that if he stood at the appropriate vantage point he would see her, providing of course that at least one of his eyes was open, that he was looking in the right direction and that he had sufficient mental faculties to recognise her and to register the fact that she was leaving the hotel at that moment.

The hotel building adjoined another building to the south; a narrow side road wound around it to the north. This did not mean that one could define the hotel as 'semi-detached' – that term only applied to dwellings, as far as he knew. What it meant, quite simply, was that, as long as the adjoining building did not provide a means of escape from the hotel via, say, a corridor through the wall that connected the two buildings, then he could concentrate his efforts on the façades of the hotel, that is to say, the western façade containing the main entry and exit point from which he had just been ejected, the northern façade fronting the side road that wound its way around the hotel, and the eastern façade at the rear of the hotel. Noting that there was a colonnaded church across from, and with a clear view of, the hotel entrance, he made his way towards the side road to investigate possible exit routes from the side and rear façades.

As he walked along the pavement closest to the hotel, he reflected that in so many cases that he, at least, had noted, planners of the modern city tried not to leave narrow gaps between buildings but preferred, instead, for buildings that were sufficiently close to each other to share a wall, as in the current case. This was perhaps to do with the fact that such gaps, rather than being called gaps, were called, in fact, alleyways, and bred (or could breed) unlawful activities which, in the absence of talented law enforcement officers such as himself, could become rife. The reason they bred (or could breed) unlawful activities was quite simple – it was because these alleyways were not generally overlooked. The current situation was a case in point: if there had been a gap between the two buildings, a so-called alleyway, then it would have made his job of surveillance close to impossible. To survey a scene, as he was just about to do (he was still casing the joint, remember, the traditional precursor to a covert surveillance operation), one needed not to be seen oneself; at least, one needed not to be seen to be conducting surveillance. People's behaviour almost always changed if they knew they were being watched. And you didn't want people's actions to be changed by the act of surveying. The reason that you wanted people to act naturally in this situation was that you wanted your surveillance, or more specifically the notes or other records, and memories, of your surveillance, to be capable of standing up in court – that was how it was put. If they, that is, your notes, records etc, could not stand up in court, then there was no point in making them, except, perhaps, to satisfy your own personal interest or curiosity, or to confirm (or otherwise) something in your own mind without wanting to convince others of that fact. In a surveillance operation that one was conducting as a means of convincing a jury or judge or both of the guilt or innocence of a suspect, say, or to provide other evidence in that court of law leading directly or indirectly to a conviction, then it was important that the suspect (or other person under surveillance) did not know that they were under surveillance. The reason for this, to summarise, was that if the person under surveillance knew that they were under surveillance then they may change their behaviour – they may refrain from undertaking the unlawful act that they had intended, an act that they would otherwise have performed quite happily, perhaps.

There are some acts that people will not perform if they are being observed by anyone; other acts are only performed by people if they are sure (or reasonably sure) that they are not being observed by a law enforcement agent. Mugging, rape and murder are examples of the former category, with cycling the wrong way down a one-way street (or down an alleyway) an example of the latter. There are various means by which one can undertake surveillance of people suspected in each category – different methods are required for each. For the latter more minor offences it may be sufficient simply to hide one's face behind a newspaper as one surveys the scene – that, at least, was the traditional method. You can, if it's useful, tear a small hole in the newspaper to enable you to observe the scene (the alleyway for instance) more easily, as long as it doesn't draw attention to yourself. Other essential accoutrements of this form of surveillance are dark glasses (except, perhaps, at night), a long overcoat (in autumn, winter and perhaps early spring) and a hat, preferably a Fedora rather than a Stetson. The hat has the added advantage of providing shelter against a storm. In the case of a heavy storm it is best to put the newspaper aside – perhaps fold it up under your arm and whistle a tune so as not to draw attention to yourself.

So much for the practicalities of surveillance. Anyone could learn from his experience in this area, Marguerite thought.

7

Having cased the rear of the hotel and observed that at ground level it consisted of a series of closed fire exit doors recessed into the façade, Marguerite found himself at the steps of the colonnaded church at the front and to one side of the hotel. He immediately noticed that the entrance to the hotel was set back from the road so as to make a space for a taxi drop off and 'kiss and ride' drive through. This meant that the left-hand wall of the adjacent building provided the boundary of the right hand side of the dropping off point for the hotel. This could be the first place where many tourists staying at the hotel set foot in the city – actually within the city limits – wherever those limits were. The main airports purported to be part of the city, but in fact they were not. The reason that they included the city's name in their name was to aid the foreign tourist – and indeed the foreign travel agent, that is the travel agent in a foreign land rather than the foreign travel agent in this land – who may not know any better. They (the foreign, or at least distant tourist) may be in their own city, town or village and want to come to Marguerite's city, or more accurately perhaps, at least to Marguerite's mind, want to come to the Mayor's city, and if the name of that city did not appear in the names of the airports that surrounded the city then it might cause a good deal of confusion in the minds of potential travellers, confusion that was dispelled by including the name of the city in the name of the airport, although this appellation did not always strictly hold true.

So it could be the first time that the tourist touched their foot or feet or wheelchair wheel or, in some cases, hand (Marguerite wasn't sure which these latter cases would be yet, but he would look into it) to the ground within the city limits. In fact it was highly likely that it would be the first time that the tourist touched their personal means of propulsion, whether that be foot or feet or wheel (in the expanded case of wheel- or pushchair or, more exceptionally, pram) or crutches or zimmer frame to the ground within the city limits. It would almost certainly be the first time that they set foot (etc) in the city if their means of travel from their point of entry to the country, which most likely would be either a port, airport or rail station, were a road vehicle – a hire car or taxi, to give the most common examples. Certainly, in the case of the latter it would be most unlikely, if they had been picked up by the taxi at the airport, port or railway station, that the taxi would have stopped to allow disembarkation between their point of setting foot (etc) into the country and the point of stepping out of the taxi outside the hotel, which would mean that their stepping out of the taxi outside the hotel (for those people staying at that hotel – other determinants would clearly become active if they were staying elsewhere) would be the first time that they had set foot in the city, at least on that particular trip to that city.

There were, though, troubling exceptions that flooded Marguerite's mind at that moment as he turned to watch a woman in a short pinstriped skirt leave the hotel. Consider, for example, this: that the foreign tourist may have arrived in the country without the cash to pay for the taxi he was taking from his point of arrival into the country (that is, his place of first setting foot, etc) to the hotel, but he may have (he *must* have) the means of securing the funds to pay for the no doubt expensive taxi into the city. And it could be that they were not a tourist but a businessman, a man, that is, who is coming to the city on business – this does not mean that this man is never a tourist or has never been a tourist in that city or elsewhere, it just means that the purpose of that trip is exclusively, or primarily, business, as he may have had to write on his immigration card, depending on which country he was travelling from and the agreements (reciprocal or otherwise) that the two countries in question had in place for such matters. It might be that the tourist or businessman would ask the taxi driver to stop at a bank or a cashpoint or a bureau de change on his (their) route into the city that morning, afternoon, evening or night time (the latter two perhaps ruling out the bank or bureau de change, given their shorter opening hours when compared to the cashpoint, if one can talk about the cashpoint as having opening hours) and that, if the cashpoint (24 hours) or bank or bureau de change (during their opening hours, which may differ as to service and to location) was within the city limits then it could be that the first step of the walk (or equivalent) from the taxi to the cashpoint (etc) would be the first step that the person had made in the city during that trip, Marguerite thought, as the woman in the pinstriped skirt passed him, with a sideways glance at him.

In the case of the hire car, it could be that the foreign visitor (to use that generic term) would make their first steps in that fine city walking across the forecourt of a petrol station (provided, of course, that the petrol station was within the city limits or, at least, that the part of the forecourt of the petrol station that the foreign visitor was walking across was within the city limits), or just simply making the two or three steps (however many it would take) to walk to the petrol or diesel pump to fill up (or less than fill up) their hire car, and it would almost certainly, almost without exception, be a car – motorcycles could not be hired as far as Marguerite knew – but *how unfortunate* bicycles *could* be – at railway stations, say – this meant much more reflection time to Marguerite's mind, more troubling exceptions. But in the case of the foreign visitor travelling with their spouse, colleague or friend, say, just to give the main categories, it could be that, in both cases (that is, the taxi and the hire car, leaving aside the other vehicles that could be hired in different locations around and within the city for the time being), that one (or more, if there were more than one person accompanying the main (if we can call them that) foreign visitor (from that party of foreign visitors – it could be that there were other more important foreign visitors setting foot, or about to set foot into the city on that day, indeed, at that moment)) of that group would be setting foot in the city for the first time outside the hotel, ie those who had not got out of the taxi to go to the cashpoint (etc) or got out of the car to walk to the petrol pump, to use just the two examples that have been cited thus far.

Some people might do like the Pope and kiss the ground as they walked down the steps from the aircraft, but Marguerite had never seen anyone do that.

For those coming by public transport, the area outside the hotel would not be the first place where they had set foot within the city limits. There were a number of reasons for this, none of which Marguerite was in a position to explore. The reason Marguerite was in no position to explore them was that Isobel Absalon had appeared in the doorway to the hotel and he needed to turn his attention back to her. He noticed immediately that she was wearing the same clothes she'd been wearing on entering the hotel. This did not mean that she had not taken her clothes off when she was in the hotel, it just meant, quite simply, that at that moment she was wearing the same clothes that she'd been wearing on entering the hotel. She was wheeling the baby in the pushchair in front of her, as is traditional, with the girlfriend that she'd met in the restaurant walking beside her. They'd turned right out of the hotel, and were now walking towards Marguerite, as he stood leaning against a pillar – without a newspaper, alas – at the top of the steps into the church. As they continued moving towards him and he slipped behind the pillar, remaining on the far side of it as they passed so that they wouldn't see him and thereby compromise his surveillance of them, he noticed that she – Isobel Absalon – had very recently been crying.

8

Marguerite thought about jumping into a taxicab and saying 'Follow those people', but he knew that just wouldn't work. The reason it wouldn't work was that, unlike most bus fares, taxi fares stretched according to distance travelled, and he estimated that his funds would run out long before they got to their destination, wherever that was. The other reason – and this was the primary one – was that they were walking and he would be in a taxi. It would mean that the taxi would be travelling at walking pace not far behind them. This might arouse suspicion. Instead he started to trail them on foot, as it is known.

He wanted to keep a respectable distance from Isobel Absalon, in particular. But how was he to judge that distance? He decided he would measure from his chest to the nearest part of her body. With sprinters, they specified that it was the chest that had to cross the line first, he reasoned, and they had sophisticated means of checking that. But what was the nearest part of Isobel Absalon, he now wondered? There were various feminine, which is to say, motherly protuberances about her body which he admired as best he could from the rear. Perhaps he should measure to one of those. Whilst he was considering this he noticed that this branch of his inquiry was having an unfortunate effect upon him: he was becoming aroused[d]. He wondered whether he felt attracted to her because she was a young mother, or in spite of that fact. It had to be one or the other, or another possibility – that went without saying. One of those other possibilities was that the fact of her being a young mother didn't enter his consciousness, at least not in relation to his attraction or otherwise to her. Whatever the trigger, the stirrings in his groin that are traditionally associated with arousal meant that if he and Isobel Absalon were a set and unwavering distance apart (give or take a few centimetres) and if the experience of apprehending her were particularly agreeable, let's say, or better – exciting or stirring – then he (or that physical part of him that responded most visibly to seeing her) would slowly move towards her; an involuntary stirring would, in short, take place in his sexual organ. Were this organ unrestrained by his trousers (or shorts) (not to mention his underwear) and, were it given full rein to do so, then it would end up pointing straight (more or less) at her face (if, in a different scenario, they were seated within touching distance of each other, say, but not too close). If they happened to be standing opposite one another, at a nightclub, say, or at a bus stop, and that level of arousal happened, then his sexual organ would point more or less straight at her stomach, if they were within touching distance that is, but not too close. These are just very rough approximations.

d. Harold Absalon's power stemmed, in my view, from having gone to the right schools, despite being from the wrong background. Going to the right schools, perhaps having the state pay for that right, had, in short, given him the right accent, the right connections. How else would he have found someone of Isobel Absalon's calibre?

They are just rules of thumb. They should be taken with a pinch of salt.

There was a thought in Marguerite's mind about the applicability or otherwise of what he now dubbed 'the Sprinter's Rule' to this situation, which will be extemporised upon more fully shortly. For the time being he continued following Mrs Absalon at a discreet distance, which he tried to keep constant by monitoring his level of arousal and making minor adjustments to his split-second location in relation to hers.

He saw that the Sprinter's Rule did not and should not apply in this case: that much was now clear to him. Where the opposite sex was concerned, if you had a rule where the outermost position of the chest (when fully puffed out, like a cockerel) was the arbiter of where one was at any instant then it could be that, when he was attracted to someone, was in very close proximity to that person, could perhaps feel that person's breath on his stubbly cheek (and did the stubble mean that he was officially closer to that person, physically speaking, than he would have been in the exact same circumstances, save for the fact of being clean shaven?) and was aroused, which, given the previous conditions (by way of recap: attraction (mutuality remaining moot), close physical proximity such that the breath of that person could be felt on his stubbly or clean shaven cheek) was near certain (his arousal) then, it would seem churlish to argue, when his penis (which, it would follow, would be more or less erect given his state of arousal, which has already been established) could at that moment, be inserted into one or other (but not more than one) of that person's numerous (numerous?) orifices, that, given the Sprinter's Rule (or whatever you wanted to call it), that he WAS NOT EVEN TOUCHING THEM – how could he be, given that his chest (including the small amount of wiry chest hair and his goose bumps if it were chilly) (and, hence, he himself) was not in contact with the woman (because, unless he was very much mistaken, it would be a woman)? The whole rule fell apart in the face of such considerations. However, he felt that all was not lost: all one needed to do, he thought, was to exclude from the rule's sphere of application those cases like the current one that involved judging the physical distance between people who were attracted to one other or, more precisely in which a man was attracted to someone (male or female). He felt sure that he could exclude as negligible the distance that a woman's mound rose, or the distance covered by her erect nipples indicating, in turn, her state of arousal. That distance in a man (or at least in this man, he thought contentedly to himself) was not negligible, could not be discounted.

He wondered why he had dubbed it the Sprinter's Rule in the first place. It was not just in relation to the apostrophe – it was the selection of the possessive pronoun, if that is what it was. Why the sprinter, then, rather than the long- or middle-distance runner, or the decathlete? The decathlete took part in ten different sports and, in each one, there was the equivalent of what he had hitherto termed the Sprinter's Rule. Granted with the throwing events, which he knew were more widely known as 'field events', there was the equivalent of the Sprinter's

Rule. Here, though, it was to do with an indentation in the ground. Were high jump, pole vault, long jump and triple jump field or track events? He would look it up next time he was close to an encyclopaedia. Indeed, were they part of the decathlon? He would look that up too. He was not sure which he would look up first; in other words he didn't know which was most pressing: the categorisation of the above-mentioned events into 'track' or 'field' or into 'decathlon' or 'non-decathlon'. It did not matter, he decided. He was just happy that there were such clear demarcations in this instance. He almost didn't need to know what they were, so sure was he that clear boundaries existed between such categories.

Satisfied with this conclusion, Marguerite looked up to see that Isobel Absalon, her friend and baby had disappeared.

9

He suspected that they'd headed down a nearby side road. He followed suit, but saw no sign of them. At the end of this road he'd expected to come upon what is known as 'a crossroads'. In fact, he noticed, as he continued to approach it, that this side road formed what is known as 'a T junction' with the busier road at the end of it. He formed a mental image of a T junction and a crossroads and compared them, to emphasise the difference between them. He instantly wondered why the latter was not called an X junction. He thought the latter was not called an X junction because it would not be sufficiently clear which limb of the X the traveller was approaching from, whereas with the T junction everyone knew, or at least assumed, that they would be journeying up the vertical stem, if one could call it that, to be presented with a choice of two directions: left or right, roughly speaking. He put to one side the difference between the printed capital, with all the flourishes at its extremities, eg T, depending on the typeface or font used in this edition, and that of the handwritten word, which would mostly (or at least often, in his opinion) consist of one straight (or thereabouts) stroke from left to right (or vice versa) followed by a downward (or, in rare cases, upwards) stroke meeting the crossways stroke at its mid-point, in other words, no frilly affectations at the extremities which might confuse the use of the letter as a simile for a particular junction. One knew where one was with the T junction, in short, or at least with the representation of it within the written and spoken language.

One may not, of course, always know where one was with it on the ground, so to speak. Even the choice between two options can be agonising when one is lost, especially when one is late for an appointment – a funeral, birth or marriage, say, or an assignation of a sexual nature, which could lead to one, two or all of the other three examples quite directly, given sufficient time. And this, of course, assumes that you know that you are on the right track, so to speak, as you approach the junction. This opens up a whole other area: if you are not sure that you are on the right track at all, it could be that you have a *third* option – that of going back the way you had come, that is, back along the vertical limb of the T – and indeed a fourth more mind-blowing option, that of being in the wrong part of town altogether, in which case the approaching T junction is almost an irrelevance, a letter floating free in an alphabet soup of possibilities bubbling up in front of you so that you don't know which way to turn. But, at least at a certain level, you know where you are with the T junction. Where you are is on the vertical limb approaching the horizontal, with the simple choice that that entails.

And that is where the use of an X for the crossroads falls down, Marguerite thought, as he continued walking down the side road. You just wouldn't know where you were with that designation. But why not the + junction to denote the crossroads? It had the same brevity and elegant ellipses as the T, but had the added benefit of the absence of the typographical flourishes that had so unsettled him in the use of the latter. It had a lot to recommend it, he thought. Was there some widely accepted rule that he was unaware of which forbade one from using numerical rather that alphabetical symbols as descriptors for types of junction? It irritated him to think that he might have missed this rule during the theory part of his driving test, or during his cycling proficiency test, or when learning the Green Cross Code, each of which took him backwards, chrono-logically speaking, through some of the stages, at least, of the transport-awareness training that he had encountered during his lifetime. He made a note to check through any notes he may have retained from such training at his earli-est opportunity.

He was by now at the end of the side road, at its left 'underarm' – that, at least, was how Marguerite had come to think of it, even though this simile fell down in numer-ous ways, which he wouldn't go into now, at least not all of them. Suffice to say, Marguerite thought, that when you hold out your arms in imitation of the T then there is the whole issue of the head to take into account, which is why this particular posture is typically called the cross, after Jesus' crucifixion, and then (a lesser point perhaps this) there's the whole problem surrounding the non-right angle between arm and torso in such a pose, although it could be argued that no T junction on the ground forms perfect right angles either. He decided to leave all these matters aside until later. But he couldn't help noticing a subtle point that had entered his mind in thinking about them. He had always thought of the cross in crossroads as being the type that one would write (in pencil, was it?) on a ballot paper. But perhaps, all along, it had been the cross of Christ that was intended when one talked of a crossroads. This, if it was the case, would overcome his earlier objection about one not knowing which limb one approached the junction from (if we are talking about the X) since it would be so much clearer with the †. But it was still problematic in relation to the criteria for selection of such symbols: could one really say that only alphabetic symbols plus religious iconography could be used in such matters? It would seem somewhat arbitrary. Nevertheless, Marguerite decided at that moment, as he crossed the side road towards the right 'underarm' of the junction, that he would write to the Mayor asking him to standardise to the symbol † henceforth in all of the Mayor's reports and correspondence, and hope that it would gain acceptance in that way. Not that Marguerite was a Christian – heaven forbid. It was just the sheer elegance and clarity of the symbol in relation to road junctions that enthralled him. A footnote to the effect that any previous Christian indoctrination should be put to one side when using the symbol in this way would not go amiss, he thought, and he would add a note to that effect to his letter to the Mayor[e].

e. You could say that Harold and I'd had a nodding acquaintance with each other before he was seconded there. Maybe he knew my name. But when I'd tried to engage him I found a distance between us. Perhaps he was ashamed of me in some way. Suffice to say that there was an unacknowledged difficulty between us from the start which became more pronounced each time we saw each other.

10

He was aware that there was a ladder of streets heading north not far from his present location. That is to say that there were two main roads heading roughly north-south in that vicinity, with roads running roughly east-west connecting them. In fact, there were more than two roads in that district heading roughly north-south with roads running roughly east-west connecting them, but for simplicity's sake Marguerite focused only on two north-south roads at a time, plus the east-west roads connecting them, and it was this somewhat narrow focus that enabled him to label those particular roads in his mind as 'a ladder'. And it was only the two closest north-south roads to Marguerite's present location that were under consideration at that moment, note. In fact, since they were one-way streets travelling in opposite directions to each other, one should, to Marguerite's mind, more strictly say that the first road on his and, he hoped, Isobel Absalon's route that afternoon, was a north-south road whereas the second road, on the far side of the ladder of roads one could say, was a south-north road, even though the latter expression was less pleasing, he thought; but that was simply the reality of it. You can picture yourself, along with Marguerite and, just in front of him, he hoped, on the ladder of roads as it were, Isobel Absalon, her friend and baby; in order to be on this particular ladder one must cross the north-south road which, for the purposes of the exercise was considered to be the first point of entry onto the ladder by Marguerite and, he hoped, by Isobel Absalon, her friend and baby. The reasons that it was considered to be the first point of entry (etc) were that: a) Isobel Absalon (with her consort and child) had been travelling due west, very roughly speaking, when Marguerite had last seen them, and he suspected that they would ultimately head towards Isobel (and Harold) Absalon's house, which was in the north-west of the city; b) the ladder was set out roughly north-south or south-north – perhaps 'both north-south and south-north' would be most appropriate here given the already established facts of the two one-way streets and their contrariwise directions of flow – across the path of the women and child in question; and c) the north-south road is the easternmost of the two main roads on the ladder. It follows from the foregoing that (to summarise), given they had taken a westerly route and that the north-south road formed the eastern boundary of the ladder of roads that crossed that route, then it (the north-south road) would be the first point of entry by anyone (including Isobel Absalon, her consort, child and pursuer) making those moves on that grid of streets on that afternoon or any afternoon, providing, of course, that those streets were there in that configuration on any given afternoon.

It might help the reader to know how Marguerite referred in his mind – and out loud if anyone had asked him (which they didn't) – to the roads that travelled east-west (and, indeed, west-east) in the ladder of roads currently under investigation: he referred to them, momentarily, as 'rungs'. In fact it was only because he didn't know what the long sections (in wood or metal) of a ladder were called – that is, those sections at right angles to the rungs – that he hadn't referred to those long sections by name; he wasn't keeping this word from the reader.

Although unsatisfied that he had taken this line of inquiry to its proper conclusion, Marguerite decided that his investigation in this regard was detaining him unduly and that he should refocus his attention more directly on his pursuit of Isobel Absalon (etc). He thought this and then he acted to pursue her (etc).

11

He turned a corner, onto the ladder of streets, noting that the first street was, in fact, two-way, at least along this portion, and immediately saw them. Isobel Absalon emerged from a shop just in front of him, followed by her child and friend, and moved across the pavement to hail a taxicab passing on the other side of the street. To be clear, the friend in question was a friend of Isobel Absalon's rather than of the child; at least, she (the friend) was *primarily* a friend of Isobel Absalon rather than of Isobel Absalon's child; this was not to say that she was *un*friendly to the child, it was just to say that: a) the child was perhaps too young to develop friendships, at least reciprocal ones, and b) the relationship of Isobel Absalon and her friend (the one in question) must, to Marguerite's mind, have started long before Isobel Absalon's child was born, meaning that it was better established, although that was not to say that quantity can be a substitute for quality in such matters. Marguerite felt that a thesis on this particular topic would make a particularly good read and made a mental note to initiate some research, some proper investigations, in this area at the earliest opportunity.

This was all, of course, predicated on the fact that the

person in question, whom Marguerite had, until then, been calling 'a friend' was indeed a friend of Isobel Absalon's. Marguerite realised at that moment that this had been speculation on his part: he had never seen the 'friend' before that day, when his investigation into the disappearance of Harold Absalon had led him onto the trail of his wife (and he let the personal pronoun slip in this instance, for the time being at least, for the sake of brevity, amongst other things that he would also not enumerate, for the sake of brevity, amongst other things, etc). The woman in question could simply have been an acquaintance of Isobel Absalon's. A further alternative was that she was with Isobel Absalon in some official capacity – perhaps she was also investigating the disappearance of Harold Absalon[f], had been sent from another agency to do so, an agency, moreover, that had not informed Marguerite's superiors (or inferiors or peers) of their parallel operation, thereby potentially compromising Marguerite's own operation, with which he had made so much headway (as he hoped was clear), especially in tracing the progress of the missing man's wife around the city in question. He realised then that he had made a big slip in his investigation by making the assumption that he'd made; he was ashamed of himself, perhaps;

f. What I found happening, after a while – and this is something that continues to perplex – was that the success of Harold Absalon's career seemed to be inversely proportional to my own; to spell it out: the more influence he had over the project, the less my own contribution was valued or even noticed. When Harold Absalon entered the office – and he continued simply to visit us from time to time, rather than having a permanent desk there – there seemed immediately to be an atmosphere of celebration, welcome, deference towards him. At the same time my colleagues, who had hitherto at least acknowledged me, even if they didn't laugh at my jokes – started shunning me, even actively ridiculing me. How would you have responded in that situation?

surprised at himself, certainly. But he realised that this slip did not completely sink his investigation – too many clues had already been amassed for that to be the case. But what he did realise was that he would have to go back through his (mental and physical) notes and amend them in the following way: wherever he saw the word 'friend' – with reference only to the woman in question, of course – then he would have to make an amendment, with the necessary signatures and counter signatures to verify his identity in doing so (to show that his evidence, in short, had not been tampered with by someone else). He resolved to refer to the woman in question simply as 'Woman A'. He looked at her more closely to double check that she was indeed female. As far as he could tell, she was. He was satisfied, finally, that in referring to her as 'Woman A' he was in line with the protocols that he had learnt during his extensive covert and overt training; for this reason he was also satisfied that all in the hierarchy of his organisation (to use that slightly shorter hand) would indeed be satisfied with him making the aforementioned amendments to his records.

But how, he now wondered, did he know the baby was the Absalons'?

12

The taxi driver did not stop immediately – that might have been dangerous; after all, hailing was very different to the emergency gesture of flagging down, as it is known (even though no flags are involved). Instead the taxi slowed down and the driver looked at Isobel Absalon quizzically through the side window, pointing in the direction he was travelling, namely south, and raising both eyebrows. He wanted, then, to know which direction she (or they) wished to travel in. Isobel Absalon pointed in a generally northerly direction and the taxi driver gave her what is known as the 'thumbs up', although only one of his thumbs was involved in this instance, presumably, again, for safety reasons. Marguerite took this gesture to mean that the taxi driver understood her indication and would turn his taxi around, assuming, that is, for the time being, that the taxi was actually his. After a short period of continued southerly travel, which allowed a number of vehicles to pass it in a northerly direction, the taxi started turning around with that impressively tight turning circle that such vehicles tended to have, at least in the city that Marguerite was then inhabiting.

Marguerite found it fascinating that there was a convention, in that situation, as in so many, which was instantly understood by both driver and potential passenger alike: the driver knew to ask the question 'which direction do you want to travel in?' if appropriate, and the potential passenger knew that there was a possibility that such a question would be asked, and that they didn't even need to be primed or prepared in any way (mentally that is), they could just respond to the question in the most appropriate manner when it arose, and they may not even have been asked the question before; in fact that might have been the first time that Isobel Absalon had been asked the question; Marguerite didn't have anything in his files on her having been asked this question in the past, he was pretty sure, which is not to say that she had not been asked the question; his files were not exhaustive. All he could say with some certainty was that Isobel Absalon had not been asked the question in all the time that he had been following her on that particular day. It is not the sort of question that one was asked without having first requested a taxi, specifically, he thought. He could not, however, rule out conclusively that she had not been asked the question when she was in the hotel with her baby and Woman A and they were having lunch. There was a 'window of opportunity' as he termed it, when Isobel Absalon et al had been in the hotel, for her to have been asked by someone (Woman A being the most likely candidate) which direction she was travelling in, perhaps when she was getting up to leave, having paid the bill. The reference to the bill raised a number of other issues worthy of investigation and resolution in Marguerite's mind, the first of which was the fact that the waiter or maître d' were also candidates in this scenario for asking

Isobel Absalon which direction she was travelling in, but only if she had requested a taxi to be ordered by them or by another member of staff at that hotel or its restaurant, thus providing the context for asking the question, a context that was immediately established in the case of the taxi driver when following a correct interpretation of a raised hand as an instance of being hailed. That was one point. The other, which Marguerite knew would have to be put to one side for now, was the similarity between raising one's hand to hail a taxi and raising one's hand, perhaps then followed by a scribbling flourish, that international call sign, that near universal signal for requesting the bill (or check). And perhaps therein lay the difference between the two: one was just a raised hand and the other was a raised hand with the addition of a scribbling flourish reflected either quizzically by the waiter or maître d' (followed by an affirmation by the customer), or performed more definitively by the customer, that is to say the diner (or recent diner, depending on how one defines them), in which case just a nod of the head from the waiter or maître d' would suffice as a response. What Marguerite realised, with relief, as the taxi pulled up, as it is known, alongside Isobel Absalon, her baby and Woman A, was that Isobel Absalon was highly unlikely to have been asked, in the restaurant by Woman A, the waiter, the maître d' or by anyone else, the question in the silent way that the taxi driver had just asked it. This satisfied Marguerite: he felt justified, finally, in asserting that it was highly unlikely that Isobel Absalon had been asked that question *in the silent way* since he had been trailing her on that particular day.

Marguerite made a brief clarification at that point, as Isobel Absalon held open the cab door for Woman A: in saying 'in the silent way' he did not mean that there was silence in the road where Isobel Absalon had hailed the taxi; the silence referred, rather, to the taxi driver's voice and, more specifically, to how much of that voice entered the hailer's (that is, in this instance, Isobel Absalon's) ears and also aural perceptions; it could be that the taxi driver had actually vocalised the question 'Which way you going, love?' or something like that, rather than just mouthing it, but if this hadn't been heard by the hailer then it could be said to be silent from the hailer's point of view. So, the clarification in Marguerite's mind was that the reference to 'silence' simply indicated that the hailer could not hear the driver's question, regardless of whether that question was vocalised or not and regardless of any other noises that were entering the hailer's aural consciousness at that moment. Marguerite felt confident enough to proceed given these important clarifications.

He then made a mental note of another convention that was inherent in this regard, as Woman A climbed into the cab. The reader will no doubt remember Marguerite's surmise that Isobel Absalon et al were moving towards Isobel and Harold Absalon's house, which was in the north-west of the city. Why, then, when asked silently (in the sense defined) by the taxi driver which direction she was travelling in did Isobel Absalon point directly (more or less) northwards? The reason for this, quite simply, was that there was a shared assumption, a tacit constraint, as it were, placed on the hailer by the taxi driver in asking this

question, and that constraint can be expressed by entering, briefly, the taxi driver's consciousness. Don't worry – it
will only be that part of the consciousness that relates to
the specific and narrow question at hand. 'In asking you
silently (etc) the question "Which way you going, love?"
I want you to limit your answer to the two directions of
this particular road along which I am travelling and, in
fact, any roads that are nearby, for example a side road
a few yards away from me, but roughly in my (and your)
direction of travel, especially where that side road may
help me to cause less disruption to other motorists (and,
to a lesser extent, to other vehicles such as bicycles, and
to pedestrians) in stopping. To relate this to the specific
example: you, Isobel Absalon,' (although the driver was
unlikely actually to know her name) 'agree to respond to
my question by either: a) pointing north, b) pointing south,
or (more rarely) c) pointing to a nearby side road that I
can easily manoeuvre into, given that the road that I am
currently travelling along is,' as was established earlier,
'a north-south (etc) road. Further, you will point north or
south or to a nearby side road regardless of whether your
destination is actually in a northerly or southerly direction
(or in the direction of the side road). In other words, your
pointing is simply constrained by the direction in which
we shall set off, rather than the direction in which you ultimately wish to travel,' which in the case of Isobel Absalon
we know is likely to be north-westerly. 'In the case of my
travelling along a one-way street with no nearby side roads
you must always point in my direction of travel; in fact, I
will always refrain from silently (as before) asking you, in

that particular instance, which direction you are travelling in, there being, in fact, no legal alternative to travelling in the direction indicated by the one-way arrow on the road sign. I don't want to risk losing my licence now, do I, love? Even though the reason I'm asking you the question in the case of the two-way street is to see whether I can do a "U"ey, providing there is not a "no U turn" sign on this particular stretch of road, so that I can help you to board my taxi by pulling up alongside you, given that, at the moment you hailed me I was travelling in the opposite direction to the one in which you were wishing to travel.' Entering the cabbie's mind had been a good form of presentation of this issue, to Marguerite's mind. But it did not help him directly in his continuing pursuit of Isobel Absalon, who was wheeling the pushchair into the cab, assisted, from the inside, by Woman A.

13

Marguerite realised, as he continued to approach the taxi, that his problem would primarily be one of transport mode: assuming that he remained at liberty to pursue it, the taxi would travel much faster than him. Taxis had motorised parts – except, of course, for the bicycle rickshaw and the gondola – and this enabled them routinely to travel faster than even the fastest pedestrian. His best hope, he realised, would be for the taxi to get stuck in congestion, as many vehicles did in that part of the city at that time, thereby allowing him potentially to keep pace with it.

Taxis did, then, travel more slowly on occasion than pedestrians. He had no doubt that Harold Absalon would have reported just this situation to the Mayor on numerous occasions: in other words the issue of there being too much traffic for much of the time in the city in which he worked, which in turn meant that one would be held up quite frequently, in a taxi, say, especially, but not exclusively, in the centre of the city. But this was not of course to say that all vehicles were held up in congestion to the same extent; bicycles and motorcycles, for instance, were narrower than most other vehicles on the road and so could often negotiate their way through congestion in a way that other, wider vehicles could not. There were exceptions to this rule, of course, even setting aside the bicycle rickshaw. One exception was the wide motorcycle – the 'three-wheeler' beloved of grebos, say – or the motorcycle with sidecar. These, being wider than most motorcycles, would be exceptions, although it was not clear to Marguerite whether the two particular examples he had just given would actually count as exceptions to the rule that bicycles and motorcycles were generally more adept at negotiating city congestion than most other road vehicles. The reason he doubted whether they were exceptions lay in a closer examination that his mind had been simultaneously undertaking; that is to say an examination that he was engaged in at the same time as he was setting out the examples themselves – it was like a nagging feeling which his mind had turned to, even though he was still in the process of setting the examples out to himself in full. The closer examination of the exceptions followed this broad sweep: firstly, looking at his category headings, Marguerite asserted that bicycles had two wheels and no motorised parts, although, granted, there were vehicles in the modern era that their owners and others would call 'bicycles', rather than mopeds, but which to Marguerite's mind at least, failed the second of his conditions for being considered as 'bicycles', namely, they had a motor. This (ie the motor) the riders would use, for instance, to propel them up a hill when the exertion of going up under their own steam, as it were, became too much. In this regard, Marguerite wondered whether Harold Absalon had ever

consulted the Mayor[g] about a standardisation of the conditions for the term 'bicycle', because, to Marguerite's mind,
these bicycles with little motors to help the rider attain the
hill were mopeds. How could they be anything else? The
people who called them bikes (that is, the abbreviated term
for bicycles) – their owners, pedestrians, even the vehicle
licensing authorities – the whole lot of them were just plain
wrong. He was prepared to go out on a limb on this one. He
didn't give a hoot about whether their speed was about the
same as an ordinary bicycle and so for licensing purposes
they were classified as an ordinary bicycle. He had already
said it: he didn't give two hoots about that. His point was
this: why (*why!?*), when there was such a proliferation of
exceptions to the numerous rules that are so essential to
the lawful day-to-day running of any modern city, would
one want to create another exception – the 'motorised
bicycle', if that is what some people called it – when there
was already a perfectly acceptable, indeed elegant, to Marguerite's mind, as well as being descriptively accurate and
succinct, term that encapsulated this case in full, with no
need for reflections, observations or pontifications of any
kind? Moped moped moped moped moped moped moped
moped moped moped moped moped moped moped moped
moped moped moped moped moped moped moped moped
moped moped moped moped moped moped moped
moped moped moped moped moped moped moped. Why

g. Whether it was to do with the downgrading of my role at the monthly
meeting, or other factors of which I was unaware, my position in the office
eventually became just untenable, largely due to Harold Absalon's presence there.

would anyone want to tamper with the sense of that beautiful term? It was beyond belief (almost).

Secondly, and more briefly, in terms of wheels Marguerite doubted whether bicycles had anything other than two (a maximum and minimum thereof). Notice how the tricycle, ie the non-motorised three-wheeler – 'the trike' – rules itself out. Only a madman would call a tricycle a bicycle, in Marguerite's view; this wider member of the bicycle family did not provide any trouble, then. Marguerite felt that the same move could be made, justifiably, for the motorised three-wheeler: he did not feel that it debased the term 'motorcycle' too much by defining the term so as to exclude anything with three wheels; and surely people were quite used to the terms 'motorbike and side car' (notice that the term 'car' naturally sneaks in, thereby immediately implying greater width and more wheels) and 'motorised tricycle' (again, implying a tapering at the front and the image of being 'stuck' in congestion).

Note that it did not matter whether a bicycle had a motor or otherwise in relation to the congestion issue. But it was a matter of principle to Marguerite, who only now realised that Isobel Absalon was staring straight at him.

1 4

Having noticed that his cover had been blown, as it's known, Marguerite crossed the road, between moving traffic, and stepped straight onto the open platform of a double decker bus moving in the opposite direction.

The gently curving stairs at the rear of the bus, which he swiftly ascended on his way to the upper deck, could not be said, except by a maniac of some sort, to consist of a spiral staircase proper; this was for the simple reason, Marguerite thought, as he moved to the front of the top deck, that they did not spiral back on themselves; that is, the staircase was one in which none of the stairs was directly above any of the other stairs. Nor did he feel entirely comfortable, he realised, as he acquired a discarded broadsheet newspaper, with the aforementioned 'gently curving stairs', for the perhaps obvious reason that the stairs themselves were not curved – they resembled, in fact, a quadrilateral with the leftmost side much shorter than the rightmost such that each of the steps could almost be said to be triangular, except that each consisted of four rather than three sides; simply put, it was a gently curving staircase that he ascended, and he would leave it at that, at least for now.

As he sat in a seat on the right-hand side next to a tall

man in a suit, he noticed a frisson, a fluttering around his heart and a sudden shallowness of breath. There were any number of physiological or biological reasons to explain these dual symptoms, but to Marguerite's mind they had an emotional cause: the bus had stopped, momentarily, in traffic; he had assumed that, despite the congestion, he would have had a clear run, that, in short, Isobel Absalon would not have had time to board the bus given the time available; his shortness of breath, the fluttering of his heart and, to add another symptom of his unease to the previous two, his sweating, spoke to him of an uncharacteristic potential error of judgement on his part. The bus rattled and rumbled as it waited for the traffic in front to move off and he wondered whether he had, in fact, been outwitted by Isobel Absalon and whether she was about to emerge at the top of the curved flight of stairs, that being a more elegant rendering to his mind of the 'gently curving staircase', to trap him on the upper deck. He wondered whether this error of judgement on his part was to do with his head being turned, as it was known, in Isobel Absalon's direction; whether, in short, Marguerite's fine investigative faculties were being corroded in some way by Isobel Absalon's allure and, indeed, whether allure could have this damp, warm quality to it. He thought that it could and he thought that she was affecting his cognitive systems in this way and he felt unable to bypass the effect that she was having upon him. All he could do, he felt, was to sit and wait for her to arrive.

15

As he waited, Marguerite reflected that the spiral staircase was never, in his experience, referred to as a flight, unlike staircases of the curved and/or straight varieties. He wondered whether this was something to do with the fact that birds and other flying creatures did not naturally engage in spiral flying, at least not of the steep variety. Spiral flight could, then, be taken to be a man-made invention – the seminal case being that of the fighter plane during the second world war spiralling downwards with inevitably a crash to ground at the end. And there were perhaps two reasons why the designers of spiral staircases had not adopted the term 'flight' in relation to their staircases with this as the model.

The first reason was that they perhaps thought that this would be the wrong sort of message to send to potential purchasers and users of the staircase in question, purchasers and users who were perhaps conservative in relation to incremental elevation devices in general having only ever seen, up until the moment of the emergence of the spiral staircase, either straight or gently curving flights of stairs. The thought that one step of this new and curved invention could be directly above another and – this is the crucial point, one that was omitted earlier on – within a few steps of each other rather than within many steps of each other, as in the case of staircases in a stairwell of greater antiquity where that stairwell is designed to transport you to the various floors of a multi-storey building, might alarm more moderate staircase-users, and use of the term 'flight' might further exacerbate this alarm. He thought, then, that the inventors etc of the spiral staircase did not wish to conjure up in the mind of their potential purchasers or users the only reference to spiral flight that they had hitherto seen, namely that of the nose-diving World War II fighter plane with its concomitant loud and, some would say, somewhat nasal whine and smoke, the 'loud and some would say somewhat nasal' only referring to the whine, note, and not referring to the smoke, although this did make Marguerite wonder whether there was a World War II fighter plane, perhaps known as the dragon, which blew flames from its 'nose', an orifice that was also, in this case alone, capable of whining, in which case the 'loud and some would say somewhat nasal' could also refer perhaps to the black – as it would be – smoke that accompanied the plane's rapid spiral descent.

The second – and more important – reason that the manufacturers etc did not use the nose-diving, spiralling World War II aircraft as a prototype for the use of the term flight in relation to their new invention was, quite simply, that this war had taken place after the invention of the spiral staircase. They couldn't wait, in short. They wanted to get their staircase onto the market immediately and if others were to be in a position to refer to it and order it, as no doubt the manufacturers wanted them to, then the manufacturers, designers and/or salesmen would need to have an agreed name for their new invention, Marguerite thought, as the bus finally started to speed up, and one that did not depend upon numerous future technological, socio-political and other factors for its emergence.

16

Marguerite felt regretful but relieved, as the bus continued to speed up and Isobel Absalon did not emerge at the
top of the curved flight of stairs to confront him. This did
not of course rule out the possibility that she was sitting
downstairs vigilantly guarding the platform, constantly
surveying it, whether covertly from behind a newspaper
with or without the aid of a cunning disguise, or overtly and
without any disguise, unless one could take her lipstick,
mascara and other make up as 'disguise'. Other alternatives for her, Marguerite thought, included hijacking the
bus, as it was known (that is 'hijacking as it was known'
rather than 'bus as it was known'). This involved taking the
controls of the bus by force or the threat of force, this latter
option relying on the imagination of the driver and perhaps
also the conductor, and then driving it to a different destination with perhaps fewer, if any, stops along the way.
It had to be a different destination, Marguerite thought,
otherwise the danger involved in the hijacking would not
be justified; in other words, if someone hijacked the
bus and proceeded to stop at all of the bus stops along
its predetermined route, then one would question their
motives and would perhaps, during your investigation

into the hijacking, ask their parents or parent, depending on whether one or both of them were alive and capable of being tracked down (as it was known), whether their son or daughter, now referred in the press as 'the hijacker', perhaps had simply wanted, as a child, to be a bus driver, and whether this early desire had been frustrated in some way during the course of the child's passage into adulthood.

Another option open to Isobel Absalon was persuading the conductor to swap clothes with her or, if he could not be persuaded, forcing him to do so, leaving him bound and gagged in the area under the gently curving flight of stairs that was ordinarily reserved for folded pushchairs. She could then move to the upper deck, although in using this formulation Marguerite was not implying that she was capable of levitation or that she would ascend in any way other than the traditional means in such contexts of putting one foot in front of and at a consistently greater height than the other on the gently curving flight of stairs designed for that very purpose. She might also disguise herself further by pushing all of her lustrous hair into the conductor's peaked cap just before finally donning it and by drawing or affixing fake facial hair in the appropriate place, 'the appropriate place' here referring to a more specific location than just 'the face' referred to in the previously referred-to adjective.

Her still not appearing at the top of the flight of stairs led Marguerite to conclude that she had either missed the bus, literally and figuratively speaking, or that she was indeed biding her time by simply waiting for him on the lower deck. He ruled out the options that involved force or the threat of force forthwith and sat, his breathing and heartbeat slowly returning to normal, whatever that meant, his perspiration remaining on his skin but not being added to significantly from his internal saline stores, if they can be referred to in this way, looking out of the window as the bus picked up speed and they left what was primarily a retail area to wind around one of the city's landmarks, through a set of traffic lights and onto a broad avenue with expensive showrooms, as they are known, to the left and a great expanse of parkland to the right.

17

He decided that if the conductor appeared on the upper deck, which traditionally they would do to check the tickets of upper deck passengers, that he would ask them whether they had 'seen this woman', as the traditional formulation would have it. Note that the tradition lay only partly in the verbal element 'Have you seen this woman?' or 'Have you seen this man?' or, probably much more often, 'Have you seen this dog?' or 'Have you seen this cat?' or, much more infrequently than the previously cited traditional examples, 'Have you seen this guinea pig?' and in the latter case the formulation would probably more likely be 'Have you seen my guinea pig?', the replacement of the definite article (if that is what it is) with the possessive pronoun (if etc), both bringing a more emotional tone to the appeal, perhaps indicative that the appeal was being made by a child, or someone child-like at least, and also capturing something of the fact that a missing guinea pig would be more unusual than a missing person or dog or cat with the recognition inherent in the unusualness of the disappearance, and the relative rarity of guinea pig as pet, that most people wouldn't be able to identify one guinea pig from another, especially given the fact that the photos involved, which are often cut from newspaper appeals, such as the one that Marguerite felt sure must have initiated the search for Harold Absalon, would generally be in black and white, meaning that any colourful markings or other distinctive features that guinea pigs may or may not have would be somewhat obscured. The traditional formulation was, then, 'Have you seen this whatever?' where the word 'whatever' is used for succinctness and should be substituted, as appropriate, with 'man', 'woman', 'dog', 'cat', 'guinea pig', 'terrapin', 'gerbil', 'umbrella' or whatever, this second use of whatever not lending itself to substitution in place of the original use of the word in the question since that would be a waste of time and would achieve nothing, and that is why the second use of the word had not been flanked by inverted commas in Marguerite's mind.

A photograph was the traditional accompaniment to this question. The formulation 'Have you seen this whatever?' would be quite meaningless, in fact, without an accompanying photograph. And it was not just any photograph that could be used to accompany the question. For instance, if one were to ask 'Have you seen this gerbil?' whilst holding out a picture of a labrador to the person that one is asking so that they can clearly see the labrador, that is, so that the photograph is face up, so to speak, and held in the direction of the viewing apparatus of the person being questioned about the disappearance (although one cannot, of course, be sure that even when these conditions are being met that the person being questioned *would* be able to see the labrador in question – they may, after all, be blind or, in the situation where the labrador has been photographed against a golden (that is to say labrador-coloured) background, colour-blind, in which latter case they would not be able to make out, perhaps, the outline of the hound against the similarly coloured background) – then that would be quite nonsensical to that person, the one, remember, who both has the wherewithal to see and is *actually* seeing the labrador in question – the *image*, that is, of the labrador in question, rather than the actual labrador, since it would be equally (more or less) nonsensical, but in a different way, to ask the person 'Have you seen this gerbil?' whilst pointing to a real labrador or hound of perhaps another breed.

Are labradors the same as golden retrievers, Marguerite then wondered? He would look into it at his earliest opportunity. Alternatively, if you know the answer and happen to be sitting next to, or near to him on the top deck of the bus pursuing what he now took to be a very warm lead (different sort) in his investigation into the disappearance of Harold Absalon, the Mayor's transport advisor, with Isobel Absalon perhaps on the lower deck, as they continued to move down the tree-lined avenue and he waited for the bus conductor to appear at the top of the curved flight of stairs and onto the upper deck, then please do tap him on the shoulder and let him know the answer, but do so in a discreet way, in other words in a way that does not blow his cover (as it is known). He thought of himself as the golden retriever of detectives, whether or not they were the same as labradors, gold signifying in his mind the best of the best, the Olympic champion investigator, and retriever indicating the retrieval of missing persons – Harold Absalon in the current case – or suspects related to disappearances or crimes – of which he was the prime exponent, as will, by now, be clear.

Returning to the case at hand: holding out a picture of one domestic or domesticated animal – or pointing to the actual animal – whilst appealing for information about another species entirely would be equally nonsensical, then, more or less. What would be even more nonsensical, to Marguerite's mind, though, would be to ask the question 'Have you seen this woman?' (to use the instance specific to his current situation of the general question that accompanied such an approach) when one didn't have any sort of photograph in one's possession to show the person that one was putting the question to. The previous cases were absurd, Marguerite now clarified in his mind, whereas this latter instance was pure nonsense. That was how he would distinguish them in the future if he were called upon to do so. Neither the absurd nor the nonsensical case pertained to his situation on the top deck of the bus, however, since he did in fact have a photograph of Isobel Absalon in his possession – a photograph of her with her baby shortly after giving birth[h] – which he could show to the conductor when he or she finally appeared at his side, if, that is, he thought this would help him in his investigation into the disappearance of Harold Absalon, the Mayor's transport advisor.

h. I took it up with my boss. I put it as plainly as I could: what has he got that I haven't? He laughed in my face, and walked off. It seemed to put him in a good mood for the rest of the day.

18

Marguerite started using the broadsheet newspaper that he'd acquired to shield his face and the parts of his body in its vicinity as he swivelled, counter-clockwise, to check whether anyone had emerged at the top of the curved flight of stairs. In order to effect this swivelling and shielding, Marguerite, who was sitting towards the front of the top deck on the right of the aisle, remember, swung his left leg out into the aisle whilst leaving his right leg wedged into the well between his seat and the seat in front. This posture, which had not been taught to him in cadet school or in any other covert or overt training environment but which he had improvised and knew instinctively to adopt in the current situation, had a number of benefits: firstly, it effected the drawing of cooler air through a gap in his left trouser leg directly to the region of his genitals which, given the fact that it was a humid day and that the window to his right remained resolutely closed (he assumed that the mechanism was stuck), brought welcome relief to this area and, by extension, to his being as a whole. This could only be held to be a side benefit of the posture, however. After all, he'd had to endure far worse conditions on operations and even on campaigns in the past. Indeed if this ventilative relief were the only benefit of adopting the posture then he would not have been adopting it, for the simple reason that the posture had a number of disbenefits, if one could call them that, which he would come onto, in his mind (of course – where else?), once he had set out the benefits of the posture more fully. Another benefit of the posture, then – and this could perhaps be held to be the primary one – was that it provided him with a firm foundation for swivelling counter-clockwise in his seat as he looked over his left shoulder at the scene at the top of the stairs, whilst shielding his face (etc). This enabled him to assess, covertly, the comings and goings in that vicinity, something he wished to do for reasons that have already been made reasonably clear.

Why, though, didn't he look over his right shoulder; that is to say, why did he not effect what was known as a clockwise swivel in his seat, given that the top of the curved flight of stairs could more accurately be said to be more directly over his right rather than over his left shoulder? His preference for looking over his left shoulder was not, he wanted to stress, so that he could refer to this part of his operation as 'counter surveillance'. No, it had more to do with the fact that he was sitting next to someone in the double seat, someone, in other words, immediately to his right whom he felt he would disturb if he swivelled clockwise fashion, especially given the clearance required by his elbows and his newspaper and the importance of the former, together with his left foot and leg in the aisle, for stabilising his posture post-swivel and of the latter as a means of disguising himself from anyone emerging from the lower deck. It was for these reasons, then, that he chose the more expansive counter-clockwise swivel to the somewhat more contained clockwise swivel, even though the expansiveness of the former had the disadvantage, Marguerite felt, of potentially drawing attention to himself.

The foot in the aisle was akin, he thought, to the extendable feet that one found on mobile cranes and other load-bearing construction vehicles and structures. He was pleased with this analogy – it seemed to capture something of the situation that he found himself in; but he would now, he felt, have to explain more fully the benefits of stabilisation feet on mobile cranes and on other tall temporary structures, such as what were known, he thought, as cherry pickers, before clarifying which of these benefits pertained to his situation atop the double decker bus.

Firstly he noted that the primary reason that such tall temporary structures had extendable legs and firm feet in this way was safety. Having legs that extended out to the side and, at the end of them, or thereabouts, feet that placed themselves, or more usually were placed by others, firmly on the ground, meant that the chances of the load-bearing construction vehicle or structure toppling over were significantly reduced. Note that in stating that the feet were placed firmly on the ground, it has been assumed that the ground beneath those feet was itself firm. Examples of infirm ground, for those who have little or no experience of it, include sand of the shifting or quick varieties, loose-fitting manhole covers, as they are known (and no doubt most men would willingly accept the blame from women for the loose fit of such covers, even if in the modern city the holes that are covered in this way are no longer the exclusive domain of men, ie some women are now known, no doubt, to emerge from such holes in their hard hats, having serviced some underground utility or other, such as a sewer, storm drain or telecommunications network), loose paving slabs or wet turf.

In his case the stabilisation provided by his left foot being placed in the aisle mainly related to making sure he didn't fall off his seat as he swivelled, which would, he thought, draw attention to himself further, thereby further compromising his operation. There was a tidy parity, in a sense, between him and all of the load-bearing construction vehicles and structures that contained stabilisation feet, in that the main purpose of the stabilisation feet was to ensure that the vehicles or structures in question also did not topple over. However, there was a key difference between him and some of these structures or vehicles: not all of them swivelled, in essence. For instance, he felt he could immediately rule out the cherry picker and the skip lorry. The reason that he could rule out these non-swivelling, load-bearing construction vehicles and structures was because he thought that the stabilisation feet used in that subset of such vehicles and structures were used only to counterbalance, if that was the correct term, the lifting of a heavy weight, whereas the use of such feet in the case of the mobile crane and other swivelling, load-bearing construction vehicles and structures must also relate to enabling them to swivel, with or without that heavy weight, in a stabilised way through a previously cleared or purposefully selected clear area. Another way of expressing this

71

was to say that most load-bearing construction vehicles and structures containing stabilisation feet did not swivel, whereas the crane, whether of the mobile or tower variety, was perhaps the entity par excellence in this class that swivelled.

The fact that the primary purpose of the crane's swivel was so as to position itself to enable it to pick something up or drop something, rather than to observe something or someone in a different direction, troubled Marguerite, as the bus slowed down to a stop at traffic lights, the redness of which was diffused in the windows of the bus and was briefly visible to him prior to his swivelling counter clockwise, once again, to peer over his left shoulder; this aspect troubled him because it did not pertain to the situation of his own swivel – he was not, in short, swivelling with the purpose of picking something up. But he left this troubling discrepancy to one side, as it were, given the sudden emergence at the end of the aisle on the top deck of the bus upon which he was travelling of the bus conductor, who happened to be a heavy-set black woman.

19

Marguerite didn't have any precise data on the prevalence of females in the city's bus-conducting workforce. In fact he had no data whatsoever in this area except, of course, for the singular datum (note) that had just appeared at the top of the stairs. But was this female conductor really the only datum upon which he could base his speculations about the prevalence or otherwise of women in this role, with girls presumably barred on account of their age, the job of conductor not really lending itself to being a Saturday job as they are known, the Saturday job being that sub-set of jobs that girls and boys from age fourteen upwards were allowed and even expected by some parents to work in, presumably so that they could earn what is known as pocket money whilst, for the remainder of what, in the adult population, would be deemed to be the working week, concentrating on their schooling? He would add this to his long list of things to look into.

Marguerite knew from previous observations of conductors, and not just on buses (but not, note, in orchestras – this was a different but related class which he would come on to), that as soon as they entered a compartment or deck they would say something along the lines of 'All tickets please!', and this was what the conductor now did. The exclamation mark indicated a certain loudness in the request, this loudness relating, Marguerite thought, not to that class of people known as fare dodgers; that is, the loudness was not designed as a warning to the fare dodger to vacate that carriage, compartment or deck to another one, that is to continue to try to dodge the conductor to avoid paying the fare; the loudness related, Marguerite thought, to trying to tell the whole compartment (etc), that is, all of the people in that compartment, whether hard or soft of hearing, asleep or awake, fare dodger or its opposite, once and for all, that she (in the current case) had arrived in their vicinity and wanted to check their tickets to ensure that her employers in the broad sense were not conveying people for free unless it was their express wish to do so; in other words, that everyone was paying their dues. Note that the conductress, as Marguerite now labelled that sub-set of conductors who are female, in collecting what was due, was not interested, for the time being, in ensuring that the bus company paid *its* dues to those, such as the bus driver (gender unspecified in the current instance), who, rather than paying their dues to travel on the bus, were *paid* dues to travel on the bus, these dues being paid as an incentive, nothing more, for that minority of bus travellers (including the conductress herself, note), if we can call them that, to perform a certain function, such as driving or conducting, to exhaust all of the possibilities in the case of buses, but not in the case of trains or orchestras (on which more shortly). She would, presumably, be interested, at some point in that week or month, depending on whether she was paid weekly or monthly, in ensuring that she was paid what was due at least to her – due, that is, to her for performing the role of bus conductress between certain prescribed hours no doubt, and on particular routes, evidently, and according to other conditions and terms, to reverse the traditional formulation of the title of such contracts so as to be able to view this title afresh, rather than the title being shrouded, somewhat, in familiarity, a cognitive coinage, that, with which Marguerite was particularly pleased.

There could, though, be a situation in which even the conductress herself was only interested in what was due to her employers, in the broad sense, rather than what was due to her; that is, she could be focused solely, within this context, on collecting fares rather than on her own wages. For the circumstances in which this could occur, Marguerite referred back to the previous situation of a girl who had not yet come of age and so was not able to conduct, even as a Saturday job. When that girl *did* become a woman it could be that her interest in bus conductressing had, perhaps through the frustration of its non-fulfilment during her formative years, turned into a passion and, to use a different term (and Marguerite was not sure, at that moment, how to express this difference succinctly), a vocation, to the extent that she would be quite content to become a bus conductress and not be paid to perform this function, such was her love of it. But was this a realistic scenario, one involving the driven, in more senses than one, female drawn to the conducting art, which it cannot really be called, Marguerite thought, except in the case of the orchestral conductor or, in even more exceptional cases than the public transport realm, conductress, of which etc, to the extent that she would do it for free or even pay her own bus fares to herself in order to increase the enjoyment even further? He thought not. And was the enjoyment taken in the job directly proportional to the number of fares taken in this way? He thought the two were related but that there were many other factors that needed to be included in the equation, factors that he wouldn't enumerate now, given the tenuousness of the first premise, that of the bus conductress working for free through her love of the job, whether or not the woman (now) in question was of independent means, as they are known, or was the daughter of the owner of the bus company, although the latter was a better circumstance for the whole scenario of free conductressing as sketched by Marguerite quite fully now, but not, he thought, to exhaustion.

20

In other words, there was more to be said about this role. The things that were to be said were clarifications of and elaborations upon previous thoughts; they were, in other words, Marguerite trying to tie up loose ends from his earlier thinking. He thought of this tying up of loose ends as a form of self-cross-examination. His thoughts would, he thought, be cross-examined at some point in the future by someone other than himself, by someone less kind to himself than himself; now, in order to prepare for this future cross-examination, he brought his mind back to a number of his earlier thoughts as a means of trying to get right to the bottom of them.

The first thought that he set out to cross-examine was that he 'knew from previous observations of conductors, and not just on buses . . . that as soon as they entered a compartment or deck that they would say something along the lines of "All tickets please!"'

Had he or had he not thought that thought previously? He had.

How did he have access to that thought again now, in exactly the same formulation (leaving aside the ellipsis)?

Perhaps he had a photographic memory. Perhaps the

phrase had been stored somewhere for easy retrieval and editing, eg ease of insertion of the ellipsis in place of a previous phrase that did not pertain to the current self-cross-examination. Perhaps he had employed an attractive (flame haired, he imagined, for some reason, not in the literal sense of flames but in the sense of red-haired) female stenographer who could somehow note down his thoughts as he thought them and could present these thoughts back to him and to that part of himself engaged in this self-cross-examination so that there was an agreed starting point for both sides in their examination, which was only fair.

Leaving aside the means by which he re-accessed his thoughts in the exact same formulation that they had been thought previously (except . . . as before), he now moved on, with the incisive precision for which he is renowned (this is still Marguerite, remember; even though we have been taken into this new form of 'dialogue', we must remember that both sides are, in fact, Marguerite, so both will be characteristic of him, both will have his investigative qualities, as, indeed, does this parenthesis), to the word 'deck' in the passage of thought quoted previously.

What was the passage again?

He was perhaps playing a trick on himself here, perhaps testing whether he could retrieve the passage for a second time in exactly the same form as that in which it had originally been thought. This he did now: he had thought that he 'knew from previous observations of conductors and not just on buses . . . that as soon as they entered a compartment or deck that they would say something along the lines of "All tickets please!"' This second retrieval perhaps prevented further challenge in this area. Perhaps he would extrapolate from there to the conclusion that he had infinite, that is, perfect repeated retrieval, at least of this phrase, putting to one side catastrophes such as earthquakes, data corruption, or typhoons for the time being.

What did he mean by 'deck' in that context?

He had extrapolated from the upper and lower deck of a bus to a generic term 'deck' in relation to public transport as a whole.

Would he hold that where a deck existed on a public transport vehicle the potential existed for the conductor or conductress to enter that deck in the way thought?

He would.

Would he include the cross-channel ferry in the class of public transport vehicle?

He could see where he was going with this: towards being cornered into a position in which he had to hold a position that said there were conductors or conductresses on cross-channel (and other) ferries and seaborne vessels. That was plainly absurd, he thought, given that one of the main actions of the conductress (etc) in apprehending a fare dodger was to eject them from the vehicle at the next stop. This was not possible in the case of such vessels given that typically there were only generally two stops in this case with an expanse of deep water in between. This was why, he now thought, that ship, ferry or boat conductors did not typically exist. He wished he had been more circumspect, in other words, in his use of the word 'deck' in his earlier thinking.

Was he saying that fare dodgers did not exist on cross channel ferries and other channel- or sea-going vessels?

Of course not. He thought that wherever a fare was due to be paid that a fare dodger would appear, given sufficient time. In fact, on reflection, the sea-going vessel was the oldest instance, he thought, of the fare dodger – there was a whole archetype of fare dodging within this mode which was so venerable that it had its own conventions and terms or, at least, term: the equivalent of a 'fare dodger' in this regard was known as a 'stowaway', and there was a venerable tradition there.

What were his grounds for holding that the sea-going vessel was the oldest instance of fare dodging?

He thought that the grounds, as he called them, included something about the size of these vehicles or vessels and the historical development of public transport. There had been no omnibuses in hunter gatherer societies as far as he knew; at least, if such public transport vehicles existed, then they were not depicted in any of the cave art of such peoples that was currently extant, nor has any archaeological evidence been found. He thought that perhaps there had not, in the olden days, been an imperative for the public to travel en masse and quickly from one pre-ordained destination to another on paying the necessary fare for the journey.

Was he content with that as a definition of public transport?

Yes. Very.

Good. He may wish to return to it later.

Fine.

Please carry on with the ... what did he call it? Disquisition?

That was acceptable. He had been saying ...

... before he'd been interrupted ...

... that he thought that there had been no imperative for public transport, as so elegantly defined, in olden times. The only exception to this had been seaborne vessels – primarily ships, which he wished now, once and for all, to exclude from the class of public transport vehicles.

Was he excluding them on the basis of them not being vehicles, as such, or of them not being public, or both, or was he taking the very much more precarious position of holding that ships could not be defined as forms of transport?

He was certainly not holding the latter position. He wished to hold both that ships (etc) were not vehicles, nor were they public in a certain sense. The non-vehicular position could perhaps be attained by holding that only those means of transportation with wheels could be classed as vehicles.

Was he saying, then, that sea-going vessels have no wheels?

Not necessarily. Just that those wheels were not used to propel the vessel in the way that the wheels of public transport vehicles were used for propulsion.

No contact, then, between ship's wheels and the surface of the water as there is between bus wheels and the surface of the road, say?

Precisely.

Can I refer, now, to Exhibit A, the paddle steamer?

Damn.

Did this not have a wheel in contact with a surface, a wheel, moreover, that was used to propel the vehicle, if he could pointedly use that term, towards its destination?

He had nothing to say to that, but no way of expressing his silence in the context except through words.

Moving on, then. Was there any steam left in his contention that sea-going vehicles used by the public should not or even could not be contained within the class 'public transport' (and he used the word 'steam' advisedly as a means of continuing to draw attention to the paddle steamer and the argument flaws exposed by it)?

Possibly.

What, then, was the difference between public transport in the sense of buses, trains and trams compared to public transport in the case of ferries, hovercrafts and catamarans? Was it simply that the former grouping included stops on which the passenger could embark and disembark whereas the latter grouping or, more succinctly, 'group' included only the singular stop which was its destination?

Possibly, although the cruise ship had come into his mind as an example of a seaborne form of (tentatively) public transport, but one that had more than one stop. Part of the pleasure, apparently, of the cruise was the fact that it took in many ports of call, as they were known, allowing the passengers to disembark and take in a casino or simply promenade or gawk at the inhabitants of the port city or town in question – to stretch their legs, as it is known. But he would exclude the cruise ship from the class of public transport for other reasons, as the conductress, seductively or otherwise, continued to approach him down the upper aisle of the bus, the lower aisle being located, as might be expected, on the lower deck of the bus.

Noted. Moving back to the main thrust (etc), he referred, now, to another earlier passage of thought, displaying again his perhaps infinite ability to retrieve such thoughts, in the absence of the previously mentioned exceptional natural disasters: he had referred previously to the bus conductress as 'datum' rather than 'data'. Would he continue to refer to her in that way given his thinking since this thought?

He had known at the time that referring to the bus conductress as a datum in this way was inaccurate or, at the very least, imprecise, implying, as it did, that she (who, at that moment, Marguerite could see, following a counter-clockwise swivel, was trying to wake up a sleeping passenger towards the back of the top deck of the bus so that she could check that passenger's ticket) was Marguerite's only experience of a female bus conductor, the only datum in this context. What he had been trying to think was that he had not recorded previous data on bus conductors in any systematic way and could not say what percentage of female conductors there were in the work force, at least the work force as directly apprehended by him in his travels around the city investigating the disappearance of Harold Absalon. He could say that there were many more conductors than conductresses, but he couldn't quantify it. He had realised this on seeing the conductress in question and it was in this sense that he referred to her as a datum rather than as part of a wider set of data: her appearance had instigated an investigation in his mind as to the precise proportion of conductresses in the bus conducting workforce in the city; in other words, in strict quantitative terms she was a recorded datum, but this did not mean that he thought that 100 per cent of the city's conducting workforce was female, nor that she was the only instance of a conductress in that workforce, those, perhaps, being the extremes of the data analysis.

Point taken. Did he take 'female conductor' to be synonymous with 'conductress'?

He did. He would use whichever term was clearest within the context of the specific thought.

So he included conductress in the class 'conductor'?

He did, provided conductor was taken in the wider non-gender specific sense.

Quite.

He had been pleased that the term 'conductress' had appeared when it had, with its echoes of 'waitress' and 'temptress'.

Let's not go into that now.

He wanted, finally, to look at a promise that had been made to come back to the question of the orchestra conductor.

He had not promised. Furthermore, he thought that the similarities (eg taking one on a journey, emotional on the one hand, and physical and perhaps scenic on the other) and differences (of say, apparel and equipment) would be quite clear to anyone who had half a brain cell in their head. He would leave it to them to work it out for themselves. He was feeling tired and would perhaps have a little rest before the actual conductress expressed the classical imperative, which, as an aide-mémoire he now repeated: 'All tickets please!'

21

The gentleman sitting next to Marguerite asked to get out. Marguerite wondered why the gentleman had not asked to get out much sooner. In fact, he was surprised that the man had not asked to get out soon after Marguerite had sat down next to him. That was, after all, what ordinarily happened when Marguerite sat down next to someone on public transport or on another form of shared public seat, such as a bench in a park or museum, gallery or public library. Depending on the time of day, people would generally stand up soon after he had sat down, and he felt that this must be to do with an unsavoury fragrance that he emitted, one that got stronger perhaps, or less savoury (which is not to say that it got sweeter), or both, as the day progressed, especially if it was a warm day, as that particular day was. Marguerite had concluded, on a number of occasions, that the odour was related to his own perspiration – he had decided that this was the most likely scenario and he would refrain, for the time being at least, from investigating other lines of inquiry in this area.

But the man sitting next to him had not got to his feet and made his excuses when Marguerite had sat down, Marguerite reflected, as he started the action of swinging his right leg out to join his left in the aisle to open up a side road for the gentleman, as he continued to refer to him, to proceed to the aisle and thence, Marguerite assumed, to the lower deck and disembarkation, rather than to a more distant and more fragrant seat on the top deck, which would have struck Marguerite as particularly heartless in that instance.

Why particularly heartless in that instance, he wondered, as his right leg continued moving to join his left, which was still in the aisle remember, this move meaning that his genitals, which had been freshened by the legs akimbo stance that was a side benefit, in a sense, of him using his left leg as a stabiliser, in effect, for the turning of his head and torso to look over his shoulder as alluded to previously, would now be encased, he feared, almost completely by his converging legs, if they could be called 'converging' when, in fact, the left leg continued moving out slightly further into the aisle as the right approached it? Marguerite was not thinking that it would have been heartless for the gentleman to take up, as it was known, another seat on the same bus on another occasion, for example on the way home from work later that day when that same bus re-emerged from the depot to convey passengers once again. In other words, in implying that it would have been particularly heartless to take up another seat on the bus, Marguerite wanted to rule out the situation of the man taking up another seat on that particular bus but after having disembarked from that particular journey. He was only thinking about the situation where the gentleman deliberately took up another seat on that bus having asked to be excused but without disembarking. Clarifying his terms in this way, almost to his satisfaction, Marguerite proceeded. The heartlessness related to having to be asked to be let out in the way described. One did not typically have to be asked in this way when sharing a bench in a park, museum, library or gallery for reasons of space: in the case of the park bench, for instance, there was generally an expanse of space in the form of the park itself for the person that you had hitherto been sharing with to enter into whilst negotiating your body, so to speak; one was not, in other words, constrained, typically, by other furniture in the way that one was on a bus, train or, in the future no doubt, space shuttle, but leaving to one side ferry, hovercraft and catamaran as still being too problematic to Marguerite's mind. The gentleman had drawn attention to himself by having to ask to be excused; this did not happen – at least not in the same way – when one was moving away from the other benches listed. In other words, your erstwhile bench companion could move away from you much more discreetly in the case of benches in the park, gallery, etc, and could thereby salve your feelings. This was more difficult in the case of the bus and other shared public seats, such as those in court, because of the need for the momentary verbal exchange.

The gentleman would need to squeeze past Marguerite; if he were then to move to a seat a few seats away, implying that he couldn't bear to be in Marguerite's vicinity any longer, then it would seem rude at least, and, as has already been noted on a number of occasions, heartless, to Marguerite's mind. And that was all he had wanted to say, or rather think, in that regard.

22

Why, he wondered, had he chosen this 'remain seated and swivel' action to allow the gentleman to get out, rather than the more traditional (and, it has to be said, more polite) action of standing up and moving into the aisle to allow the gentleman the room to move into the aisle himself and thence to any location he chose (within reason)? In launching this inquiry into his actions during those split seconds, Marguerite had no preconceived verdict to hand down – he did not know why he had chosen this course of action over the other course outlined. It would be a poor substitute for justice if he did pre-judge his investigations in this way. He knew which questions to ask, then – the questions, in short, that he believed would lead him to unearthing the circumstances (etc), and he believed this to be one of those questions, the investigation into which, in short, would lead him a step closer, so to speak, to unravelling the twisted web of clues leading to Harold Absalon. Having moved through such thoughts as a preamble to substantive investigations in this area, he moved on to what he hoped would be substantive investigations in this area.

He didn't want to draw attention to himself for what he hoped by now were obvious reasons. He feared that standing up in the aisle and folding his newspaper noisily under his arm like a disgruntled city gent would draw attention to himself. Given these premises, the conclusion should be clear to anyone with even just an elementary schooling in the classics, he thought, as the gentleman in the seat next to him started to stand, gripping his umbrella in his right hand with his newspaper, whilst his left hand gripped the back of the seat to help effect his ascent into the standing posture. Marguerite wondered, also, whether having focused so much attention on the function of his own left leg as a fulcrum – yes, that was surely the word – that it was a natural extension in reasoning and in bodily action for his right leg to attempt to join it. In other words, perhaps it had been a rather unthinking instinctual response given what had gone before for Marguerite to swing his right leg out to meet his left having heard the words 'Excuse me, please' from the gentleman sitting next to him. Some observers – rookie recruits, say, watching Marguerite's recorded (for training purposes) actions on the surveillance cameras that the bus must contain, or which one of his fellow passengers engaged in counter surveillance may have in the peak of their cap or in the right arm of their spectacles or in their newspaper, may comment on the situation in this way, but Marguerite would not countenance it; any rookie who came to this conclusion whilst watching the master in action in this way during their training would be failed, certainly if Marguerite himself were their examiner and hopefully too if one of his trusted lieutenants following clear guidelines that Marguerite had himself lain down were the examiner. It was the word 'unthinking' that Marguerite particularly objected to. The detective must *never* be unthinking. One's quarry was always trying to outwit one and one must always have all of one's wits about one if one were to succeed. That is what he would tell the rookie who he was sending down. It might be the most useful life lesson that they would ever receive or it might not be.

Having ruled this out as an alterative, he pondered other alternatives. Another alternative was that the gentleman sitting next to him was an inept functionary of Isobel Absalon. The word 'inept' was used advisedly here. Marguerite's thinking was that perhaps Isobel Absalon had been able to communicate with this gentleman in her employ (and notice how the word 'gentleman' takes on a different hue when associated in this way with being in the employ of the tantalising Isobel Absalon) and had informed him of the presence of Marguerite on the top deck (of only two, note; he preferred 'upper' to 'top' deck for this reason ie that it was less liable to mislead people into thinking that there were intermediate floors between 'bottom' and 'top' decks), perhaps by speaking into a microphone placed discreetly on or just inside the lapel of her upper garment, whatever that was, a microphone that transmitted her whispered utterances into the ear of the upper deck functionary, the right ear, note, which had not been visible to Marguerite since it was the ear that was on the window- rather than the Marguerite-side of the seat that he had shared with the suspected functionary. Would he not want to check whether an earpiece was visible in the ear of the suspected functionary and wouldn't standing up in the aisle in the classical way allow him to make such a check? No on both counts. He didn't want to check because he felt that he wouldn't be able to check without drawing attention to himself, as it was known, and even if he did want to check, he knew that any functionary worth his or her salt, if that was the correct expression, would have discreetly dispensed with the earpiece long before saying 'Excuse me, please' in the way described and getting to their feet, as it was known, thereby potentially exposing the ear in question to surveillance and to counter surveillance, counter counter surveillance, counter counter counter surveillance and so on. So he did not want to check whether there was an earpiece of this sort in the 'shadow ear', as he now referred to it, of the suspected functionary of Isobel Absalon who had now reached his full height, and was preparing to move past Marguerite and into the aisle, if any preparation were needed at that moment in that regard. Marguerite had in fact judged that it was better to turn away from this gentleman, just as he had turned away to look over his shoulder to observe the top of the stairs, rather than turning towards him, as standing up in the aisle in the classical way would surely have ultimately entailed. The reason he had made this decision was, in short, to ensure that his face was averted throughout from the gentleman's gaze on the basis (and this is described extensively in the training manuals) that one often could not see what was right under one's nose.

23

Marguerite decided to follow the gentleman now, in an attempt to effect the following results: firstly, he wished to brush past the conductress, thereby effecting slight but definite bodily contact with her; that is, he wanted his physical body to be in contact with her physical body under the auspices of trying to squeeze past her, as it was known, down the aisle on the top deck of the bus following the gentleman's lead. The second of his mission aims, as he now thought of them, in moving past the conductress, was to move past her without paying his fare, using the man as 'cover'.

There were no ticket barriers on buses, he reflected, at least not in the sense that there were ticket barriers at train and underground stations. However, there were clear similarities between the situation that Marguerite found himself in at that moment, atop a double decker bus following a man who was approaching the conductress. One of the similarities was that the conductress could act, in a sense, as the gatekeeper even though, as has been stated, there was no gate in the sense that a ticket barrier at a train or underground station could be seen as a gate designed to keep those who haven't paid from passing through it.

She could, if she chose, act in this way. She could even act
as the gate itself, perhaps indicating that she was taking
on this role by lowering her arm in front of the first passenger hoping to disembark, that is, the gentleman who
had just got up from his seat[i], in imitation of a barrier. It
would be more reminiscent, Marguerite thought, of a road
rather than a train or underground barrier; on reflection
he wasn't sure why he had thought this – it was perhaps
to do with the fact that road barriers, in his experience,
were long and thin, reminiscent, in a way, in other words,
of the arm of the average human female, although the
differences between female arm and road barrier were
also manifold. One typical difference was that the typical
female arm tended not to be striped and certainly was not
striped, as far as Marguerite could see, in the case of the
bus conductress, whereas the road barrier did tend to be
striped – to make it more visible, he thought. Note that the
stripy long-sleeved female pullover (or other striped long-
sleeved upper body garment worn by girls or women) with
the sleeve perhaps momentarily pulled over the hand in
question could resemble, pretty well, the road barrier, but
this confluence of circumstances (the female wearing such
a garment with the end of the sleeve pulled over the hand
on that arm, which, just at that moment she wished to use
in a way that imitated a road barrier) was exceptional and
unlikely, Marguerite thought, to occur whilst he was still on

i. The proverbial straw came before the monthly meeting. As I took my seat
I could sense an air of uneasiness in the room, rather than the normal pre-
meeting bonhomie. I could sense Harold Absalon's presence beside me as
I was taking my papers out of my briefcase. Looking up, I could see that he
was waiting to take my seat, with a broad, unapologetic smile on his face.
My seat!

the bus; he therefore dispelled it from his mind, if dispel is the correct term in this situation and, further, if it can be used in this way as a verb.

So much for the similarities between the female arm, under certain conditions, and the road barrier. The main difference, to Marguerite's mind, between the two was that the axis of operation of the road barrier was from the vertical (some would say 'erect') to the horizontal (no-one would say 'flaccid') whereas the female arm would be tempted to remain – rather the female mind would be tempted to keep the female arm (one and the same female, this is) – in the horizontal plane whilst traversing, that is swinging around rather than down, ninety degrees, just as, note, the barrier at an underground or train station would tend to open and close. The reason, presumably, that underground and train barriers opened in this way rather than in the same way as a road barriers was to avoid hitting someone on the underside of the chin; similarly the reason they closed in the way that they did rather than in the way that road barriers typically closed was to avoid the equally dangerous and perhaps fatal smack on the head. There were similarities, in other words, between the female using her arm as a ticket barrier, and the action of both the train stroke underground and the road barrier. No doubt these could be explicated more fully. However, Marguerite, for the time being, was preoccupied with hoping that the conductress did not detain him or the man in front of him as they moved towards her. The reason that he hoped the conductress wouldn't detain him or them in this way was that he thought it would jeopardise his two mission aims:

he was hoping to disembark without paying, remember, given the shortness of his funds; secondly, he thought that if the conductress chose to use her arm in this way then it would reduce Marguerite's chances of squeezing (or, at the very least, brushing) past her and gaining, momentarily, definite bodily contact with her, something that was wholly unlike the experience of contact with the mechanical form of ticket barrier that one typically finds at the rail and underground termini and at intermediate stations within the city in which he was currently located and no doubt in other towns and cities in the rest of the country, in other countries within that continent and, indeed, on other continents.

Another reflection related to the term 'brush with', which, as most people will probably understand, typically goes with 'the law' as in 'brush with the law'. Did he see the conductress in this way, ie as 'the law' within the constrained context in which he was currently located? If so, did this add a frisson of excitement sufficient to take his mind from the charms of Isobel Absalon who could, at that moment, have been making her way to the top deck? He thought the answer was yes to both questions. In fact, in answering 'yes' to the latter question he thought that he would, by implication, be answering 'yes' to the former and so, for reasons of brevity he answered simply 'yes' to the latter and left the reader to work out for themselves what his sotto voce reply to the former would have been.

The classical 'brush with the law' did not, he noted, as he approached 'the law of the bus', that is (for the hard of hearing) the conductress, involve actual physical contact;

at least in his experience it did not involve actual brushing, in the way that he soon hoped to be brushing up against, or simply against, the fragrant (he assumed) law of the bus, meaning (for the partially sighted, this time) the bus conductress.

24

Marguerite paused, momentarily, in the aisle, to allow a trim, well-dressed woman to enter it from his left. The woman had been sitting on the side of the two-person seat next to the aisle, which meant that there was no intermediary between her and Marguerite, in the sense that, in the situation where she had been sitting on the half of the seat next to the window on either side of the bus, as in the case of the gentleman who had been sitting next to Marguerite, and if the other, aisle side of the seat had been occupied by someone then, in effect, that person might have had to act as an intermediary between the woman and Marguerite, assuming that they actually exited their seat and moved into the aisle, which Marguerite had chosen not to do, for the reasons previously stated, in the case of his own erstwhile 'neighbour', to allow the woman in question free passage in the sense of freeing up space for her to exit from that shared seat area rather than free in monetary terms since there was no part of the bus that counted as being

j. I have replayed that scene over and over in my mind, running different permutations of what I could have said to him. What I actually did was hurriedly gather my papers together, put them under my arm and leave the meeting in abject humiliation. The door was slammed behind me and I could hear roars of laughter at some derogatory quip that he'd no doubt made about me after I'd left.

exempt from paying the requisite fare, unless one included the driver's cab, which Marguerite did not, dismissing it in his mind as a 'non-public' or 'restricted' area. The person, then, who had hitherto been sharing the seat with the woman, if they were schooled in the traditional way for that part of the world, would have put themselves out, so to speak, particularly if they were a gentleman, that is, into the aisle down or perhaps up which Marguerite had been making steady and even speedy progress, would, in other words, depending on the timing, and on gender differences and other demographics, put themselves directly in Marguerite's path, with or without Marguerite's permission, to enable the luscious lady who, although he (the sharer) was not then sharing a seat with was still sharing the space between seats with and could therefore still, conveniently, be referred to as 'the sharer' – in fact both the intermediary, as he has also been referred to, and the woman in question, as she (etc), could both, to Marguerite's mind, be referred to as 'sharers' up until the moment that the intermediary entered the aisle, in which case Marguerite would recommend referring to them both as 'erstwhile sharers' – to exit.

To recapitulate: the most important conditions for the sharer nearest to the aisle to lend themselves to being referred to in this way as an intermediary were: a) an indigenous (to the isles or part thereof that constituted the country in which the action was taking place), traditional schooling, meaning they would momentarily relinquish their half of the seat completely to facilitate egress from that specific area rather than leaving their backside planted and swivelling in their seat, as was the continental fashion sometimes adopted, now, to Marguerite's disappointment, by the inhabitants of the isles (etc) in question (including, of course, himself, for his own reasons) and, b) an exchange, whether verbal or non-, between said intermediary and the person approaching them down the aisle – Marguerite in the case currently under investigation.

Note that in saying, or thinking, that the woman had been sitting on half of the two-person seat, that this was only a very rough measure. The actual proportion of the seat occupied depended, in part, on the size of the backside; whether or not her legs were splayed or, in the more usual, demure, fashion for women, more or less together; whether her elbows were more or less tucked into her body (the rest of it, that is); whether her hands were clasped together or resting on her legs or otherwise in close proximity to each other; and whether her torso was either leaning away from the occupant of the other half (etc) of the seat or was more or less upright, that is, not leaning excessively in the direction of the other person with whom she had been sharing a seat.

But given that the woman in question had not been sharing a seat with anyone prior to entering the aisle and, in any case, had been sitting in the aisle seat, there was no intermediary in the situation currently under investigation. It could not, note, be said that 'she acted as her own intermediary' for what Marguerite hoped, fervently, would be obvious reasons. Despite not being able to use this epithet, at least not in the narrow context currently under investigation, there had been an exchange, note, between the woman in question and Marguerite. He had instinctively indicated by an almost imperceptible pause before crossing the area of egress from the seat that she had hitherto been occupying (alone, remember) that she could move into the aisle ahead of him; the recognition that this could help him by providing further cover for his own exit from the bus had been a secondary concern, albeit one that followed immediately after his chivalric impulse to set the fair maiden free. In fact she was a brunette. It depends on how one interprets the term 'fair': briefly, it could be taken to mean internally pure and unstained; Marguerite left it at that for the time being and probably for ever.

He had waited instinctively for her to enter the aisle in front of him, not, then, just because his detecting textbooks would advise this as the favoured manoeuvre in that situation since it would provide what is known as further 'cover' for his operations along the top deck of the bus, but initially purely for reasons of chivalry. In other words, even though he knew that following close behind this woman as she moved towards the conductress was the city sleuth's textbook solution par excellence in this situation, he had only realised this after his instinctive deferral to the woman on the grounds of being a gentleman. He could see that his grounding in the investigative arts seemed to slip, in other words, in preference to a softer, more gentlemanly pre-existing training.

His investigative instincts had, in fact, let him down in this instance. The softening of his approach and his regression to a non-urban middle age (in the historical rather than personal sense) had backfired. He knew it had backfired because he had an almost imperceptible and immediate sense that the woman whom he had made way for had recognised him. Now, following closely behind her, he had an almost tangible sense that she was, as speedily as possible, accessing her possibly capacious cerebral reels (to borrow a term from one of his superiors), trying to put a name, as it was known, to his face.

25

It wasn't like the three of them – Marguerite and his two fellow passengers – were a tidy line. Nor, in a sense, were they really a ragged line. They weren't really a line at all, was what he was thinking. They were three individuals, a group, one could say, of individuals, two of whom perhaps knew each other; this 'each other' he inserted on the basis that if the woman in front of him knew him then surely it was likely that he also knew her. Surely the reciprocal relation of knowing would pertain in this context. What conditions would be needed for it not to pertain, he pondered, as, continuing to follow her, he looked at her backside moving in its short, snugly fitting, blue pinstriped skirt?

He was not famous, as far as he knew – and surely he would know if he were famous. It would have to be a very particular kind of fame for him not to be aware of it, surely. But he was, he thought, well known. In fact, he realised, as he looked down at the woman's shapely legs moving below the skirt, he was well known for having avoided fame throughout his illustrious career. Part of the name that he had made for himself, then, related to the fact that no-one truly knew him and part of what they didn't know was his name. People respected the fact that, for someone so effective in his investigative approaches as Marguerite was, so few people knew about him. That was what he had made his name for; that and his thoroughness. In fact it could be said that his thoroughness and his discretion, if we can use that latter term, were one and the same thing in that it was his thoroughness as applied to keeping a low profile that had resulted (with other factors of course, which he cannot go into now, despite his thoroughness) in his making a name for himself. That so few knew this name did not mean that it hadn't been made. What he was struggling with here, as may be apparent, was the colloquial use of the term 'making a name for' (and could that phrase be said to have anything but a colloquial use?) and the fact that very few people really knew him or his name. The distinction Marguerite then made in his mind was another master-stroke, he thought, another way in which people following in his footsteps, as it were, would henceforth try to emulate his every investigative move: one *could* make a name for discretion in this way – there were precedents in this, was what he was saying; just look at the Scarlet Pimpernel, surely the epitome of discreet notoriety. Marguerite knew that he did not exceed the Pimpernel – if he thought that he did then he would have said that he epitomised this discreet notoriety and the Pimpernel would refer to himself as being nearly as discreetly notorious as Marguerite. There was, of course, one key difference between these two undercover agents, though, which was this: Marguerite was working for the good whereas the Pimpernel worked on the side of evil; that, at least, was Marguerite's recollection of the Pimpernel, not that he had ever met him of course (and if he had, he may not have known that he had).

Were the woman in the pinstriped suit to be correct in thinking that she *did* or *does* know Marguerite (and he had the sense, as he continued to follow behind her, that she was still racking her brains, as it was known, to try to place him, as it was known), then Marguerite was holding that, given that he wasn't famous, but was, in fact, well known for not being recognisable or famous, then it was likely or, perhaps, extremely likely that he also knew *her*.

A number of premises had stacked up; these Marguerite took as a starting point for this part of his investigation into (etc) but it did not follow that he held these premises to be true; in other words, he was moving or had moved into a part of his investigation that required him to hold, momentarily, a set of assumptions to which he had not and perhaps would not subscribe until, perhaps, the final analysis, until, in other words, Harold Absalon had been found and had been returned to his beloved (another assumption) Isobel Absalon[k], assuming that this would be the end of the analysis and that the premises that Marguerite was momentarily holding to be true, at that moment of following behind a man and a woman on the top deck of a bus as they collectively moved towards the conductress who, note, was also moving towards them with a slow side-to-side action governed more by the location of passengers on either side of the aisle than by the swaying of the bus,

k. I finally resolved to do something about him. But before I could act, he followed me into the washroom – this was a few days later. As we stood beside each other, he asked me, in a quiet, conciliatory voice, whether I would do him a favour. I didn't respond, but after a while he simply said to me: 'Follow my wife.' That was what he said. 'Follow my wife.' I swear.

more accentuated on the top compared to the lower deck, as the bus slowly slowed down again with what one could call a mournful sigh of the brakes, even though this, clearly, would be an anthropomorphic projection onto an inanimate (in the absence of human operation) object, were (that is, the premises that he was metaphorically holding as he followed behind, etc) indeed true. The premises, by way of recap (etc) were, succinctly, that: a) the woman that Marguerite was following behind knows (or is it 'knew'?) Marguerite; b) Marguerite was well known for not being famous, and c) only famous people could have found themselves in a situation where they were known by someone whom they do not know themselves. A dictum emerged which encapsulated succinctly his line of reasoning: 'The famous are those people who defy empirical reciprocity.' He didn't know whether the dictum was true even given the premises; further, he wasn't sure that he was capable of having the thought as it was finally expressed. Nevertheless, the conclusion that he drew from the surprisingly short, given the foregoing thought processes, list of premises, and the even shorter, and possibly unlikely given the range of his previous thought processes and mental vocabulary, dictum, was that he knew (etc) the woman that he was following behind, the woman, in short, who had appeared to recognise him. That was how he had got to the conclusion, in short.

He hoped that his conclusion in this area was sufficiently clear, now, for him to proceed with other areas of this part of his investigation, leaving aside, that is, questions of what it really meant to be famous in the sense that he had used that term; what it meant, also, to be known or well known; thirdly, what one meant by the word recognition; finally how these three terms related to each other, what it meant, for example, to know a famous person exclusively by means of their fame, that is, assuming that one wouldn't know them, so to speak, if they were not famous; what it took to be well known without being famous or recognisable, as in Marguerite's case; whether this was even possible, or whether it was based on a misreading of one or more of the terms; these and other matters he would leave to others – his subordinates, peers, superiors or, indeed, any other enthusiast who perhaps didn't fit into any of the preceding categories – to look into, so that he could concentrate, once again, on the more principial aspects of his investigation into the disappearance of Harold Absalon, the Mayor's transport advisor.

26

Marguerite took it to be self-evident, as the gentleman in front of him came within touching distance of the conductress, that the Mayor would not want his advisors constantly to provide advice to him relating to their specialist areas. The Mayor would surely become quickly overwhelmed if this were to be the case. But at the other end of the scale, surely there was a minimum amount of advice that an advisor had to provide in order to remain an advisor and, if so, how was this minimum to be agreed and measured, Marguerite wondered, as the gentleman paused, inexplicably, before the conductress, leading Marguerite to question whether actual physical contact with her would be possible in their passage past her? And what could it mean to remain the Mayor's transport advisor when one had disappeared – as in Harold Absalon's case – and, for this reason, not to be providing any advice relating to one's specialist area – transport in Harold Absalon's case – to the Mayor?[1]

But what if Harold Absalon *had* been providing transport advice to the Mayor since his disappearance? What if the Mayor had been dissatisfied with the amount of trans-

1. No-one else was in there. After we'd washed our hands, side by side, he gave me that photo of her. Something I'd always wanted. It was so simple. And then he was gone.

port-related advice hitherto provided to him by Harold Absalon in his advisory capacity, and had incarcerated him in City Hall to encourage him, in more or less subtle ways, to provide a more continuous stream of advice as befits a more literal interpretation of the title Mayor's transport advisor? That would certainly provide a much more difficult mission brief for Marguerite in his investigation into the disappearance of Harold Absalon given that he felt that this mission had been set, albeit indirectly and without clear written or verbal instructions, by the Mayor, in that the Mayor, as well as looking after, in a sense, the transport networks in the city, at least those networks that belonged, in a sense, to him as Mayor, which was the majority of them, also oversaw, sometimes in a literal sense (for example, when viewing CCTV images at headquarters), the city's police force and a number of other law-enforcement agencies; not that the members of the city's police force and the other law-enforcement agencies within the Mayoral remit were the only investigative officers operative in that city, of course – there would also be national, extra-national (whether diplomatically friendly or unfriendly), intra-national, perhaps, and international forces in operation in the very city that Marguerite was located in at that moment. Given this dual transport/legal role that the Mayor had, which, of course, did not exhaust all of the Mayoral functions by any means, Marguerite felt that it would make his investigation significantly more difficult if the scenario pertained in which the Mayor had unlawfully detained Harold Absalon in City Hall or elsewhere as a means of obtaining a more or less constant stream of transport advice – transport advice on tap, so to speak – based on this narrow interpretation of the role envisioned, perhaps mistakenly, by the Mayor. The reason that it would make Marguerite's investigation significantly more complex and difficult was that it would entail a covert investigation of his superiors, one that he would be prepared to make for the sake of justice and transparency; but, in short, if he couldn't take the counsel of his superiors as more or less read, it would leave him even less firm ground to stand upon than he currently had. It would involve, in theory, a perhaps infinite regress of surveillance and counter surveillance, a situation that has been alluded to earlier in a somewhat different context.

But Marguerite took this scenario to be highly implausible. Marguerite was devoted to the Mayor, and refused to believe that he would act in this way. He had only entertained this scenario to limn its implications in relation to what it meant to be an advisor to the Mayor. He had rehearsed the situation of a possessive Mayor thirsty, so to speak, for advice, as one theoretical extreme, one that he thought highly unlikely to obtain in the practical, that is real life, investigation that he was engaged in.

The other extreme – that of the Mayor's transport advisor providing *no* advice to the Mayor on transport matters – he took to be more or less equally implausible. But wasn't this the situation that did, in fact, obtain at that precise moment in relation to Harold Absalon, he wondered, as the stand-off between the gentleman and the conductress inexplicably continued, whilst Marguerite and the woman in the pinstriped suit continued to approach them? This

assumed that Harold Absalon had not just gone undercover into and onto those city transport networks that were
part of the Mayoral remit in order to provide covert advice
to the Mayor. But what would be the purpose of providing advice in this way, Marguerite wondered? When the
supervisor appears on a factory floor then it is perhaps
probable that productivity goes up, thereby precluding an
accurate assessment by the supervisor of the productivity
of the factory workers in that instance. Could it be that the
Mayor had sent Harold Absalon underground in more than
one sense to provide what he hoped would be an objective
assessment of how efficiently the city's transport networks
were operating, an assessment, in short, that could not be
made by Harold Absalon under normal circumstances,
whatever that means, given the modicum of fame and
notoriety that he had as the Mayor's transport advisor? In
other words, the drivers, conductors and conductresses,
including the one that Marguerite fervently hoped to make
actual bodily contact with before too long, might change
their behaviour if they knew Harold Absalon and saw him
on their particular bus, train, tram, taxi or boat (leaving to
one side, yet again, and regretfully to Marguerite's mind,
what, precisely, constitutes public transport and what does
not), thereby preventing Harold Absalon from obtaining
objective data on their performance, which, in turn, would
prevent him from providing reliable advice to the Mayor
relating to the city's transport networks. Was it this, then,
that precipitated Harold Absalon's 'disappearance' – a
desire to travel the city undercover so as to provide more
reliable transport-related advice to the Mayor, advice

that had hitherto been unavailable to the Mayor given the modicum of fame that his transport advisor had obtained qua transport advisor? Under this scenario it should be clear to almost everyone with access, in this mysterious way, to Marguerite's thoughts, that Harold Absalon would have remained the Mayor's transport advisor despite even protestations to the contrary by the Mayor himself and/or by the Mayor's spokesman or -woman (who, note, would remain the Mayor's spokesman or -woman, just as Harold Absalon would remain the Mayor's transport advisor under certain circumstances, even if he or she did not speak on behalf of the Mayor or anyone else – indeed even if they refrained from speaking at all – for some period of time, still undefined, for what could actually be quite a long period of time, such as a month or two or even, at a stretch, a year, given certain conditions, that is), the protestations to the contrary by the Mayor and his coterie, that is, including his spokesman or -woman, being a mere smokescreen, perhaps, created to ensure that Harold Absalon remained incognito on the city's streets, trains and buses, etc.

The reason that Marguerite felt this new scenario unlikely to obtain related to certain key differences between workers on shop or factory floor and transport workers on the city's streets, rails and waterways, if the preposition can be followed through elegantly enough, perhaps, in that way. Marguerite was aware that there were certain key distinctions between the two work environments, as the conductress and the gentleman loomed larger and larger, just in perspectival terms, that is, rather than in actuality. The key distinction related, he thought, to the level of control over 'output' that the factory worker had compared to the transport worker. There were, in short, many more factors beyond the transport worker's control in relation to their efficiency than there were in the case of the factory worker. Take, for example, the issue of congestion or signal failure. Were the transport worker's supervisor, operating under- or overcover, to discipline the transport worker for not meeting their timetable slot under conditions of signal failure or excessive congestion, then that could be taken to tribunal, to Marguerite's mind, by the transport worker and could be held up as being grossly unfair, he thought. The equivalent in the factory of chatting too much, say, and this slowing down the work, or of being too hungover to complete one's tasks for the day, would be quite different and might more appropriately be treated as a disciplinary matter given certain other documented or verbally expressed previous warnings which, in turn, depended on other, relatively tightly defined circumstances. In short, it was much easier for the factory supervisor to judge of those inefficiencies that were the responsibility of the worker rather than due to external (to the worker) factors than it was in the case of the transport supervisor, if, indeed, such an operative existed. A whole new field of inquiry emerged into Marguerite's mind then; this related to covert action on behalf of the employees relating to their working conditions, rather than by the employers in relation to the employee's working efficiency. He refrained from looking into that area at that moment, interesting though it seemed, given that the gentleman in front of him was involved, finally, in squeezing past the conductress, with all that that implied.

27

The bus continued to slow down, the woman in the pinstriped suit continued moving towards the conductress,
and Marguerite feared, now, that he would still be on the
top deck after the bus had stopped. There were a number
of reasons that he feared this. Before he went into these
reasons he wanted to make a distinction in his own mind
in relation to the word 'feared': its use in the context of
'fearing that he would still be on the top deck after the
bus had stopped' had at least two interpretations and he
wished to be clear that he did not mean to use *both* of them.
In fact, he wouldn't prejudge the number of different interpretations, meanings or definitions of the verb 'to fear',
provided the number of interpretations (etc) was a whole
number greater than one; that is, if further emphasis or
clarification of this point is needed, which it is not, a whole
number greater than or equal to two. This caveat was necessary, to Marguerite's mind, because he had said that he
wouldn't prejudge the number of available interpretations
of the verb 'to fear' in this context, whilst at the same time
being aware of two such interpretations. Two, then, was
the absolute minimum number of interpretations that he
would countenance; anything above that he had an open

mind towards. His open mind only extended, however, to the possible existence of more than the two interpretations of the verb 'to fear' that he was aware of; it did not extend to him accepting that he was actually experiencing fear in these tertiary, quarteriary (if that was the right word) and higher (or wider) senses of the word. All he was prepared to concede, in this latter instance, was that he was experiencing fear in terms of the variant of the verb that had initially come to mind.

The variant of the verb that had initially come to Marguerite's mind was fearing in the sense of just worrying that he wouldn't be able to get off the bus at the next stop given the speed at which he was journeying behind his two co-passengers compared to the rate at which the bus was decelerating. He was constrained, of course, by the speed at which his fellow passengers were moving in front of him. He wondered, now, whether they were planning to disembark at all or whether they were hoping to disembark after the next stop, thereby blocking Marguerite's disembarkation at the next stop and impeding his investigation, a criminal act that he couldn't warn them of given the covert nature of his operation.

The first sort of fear, Marguerite now realised, could be held to relate, quite simply, to the fact of one's missing one's stop; that is, it could be held to be a generalised anxiety about missing one's stop, without any specific object, without, at least, any conscious specific object for the fear to attach itself to, as it were; the second type of fear related, he felt, to the *consequences* of missing one's stop which, in his case, ranged, he thought, from feeling exposed, potentially, to the wrathful gaze and, he suspected, malign intentions of Isobel Absalon, who he feared was still lurking on the bottom deck[m]; or to whatever the woman in the pinstriped suit might do to him having had sufficient time, given the respective speeds alluded to earlier, to put a name to his face, as it is known.

He noted that the classical situation that he was alluding to – that is, the classical situation within which these initial two variants of the verb 'to fear' are used in this context – consisted of the disembarkation concerns of an elderly person, perhaps not seated, for whatever reason, in the seat or seats designated for their use, which was or were almost always near the door or, in the case of the bus that Marguerite was travelling on, near the platform from which one disembarked and onto which one embarked, that is, the seat or seats that are classically designated for them as a means of helping them to overcome just this sort of fear.

There was a third kind of fear that came into Marguerite's mind at that moment, and which perhaps related to the previous two types, especially in the classical case of the elderly person (as before): this was fear of physical harm, which could come about in a number of ways. One way in which actual physical harm could come about in this context, thereby justifying the pensioner's or other person's fear, was the unfortunate case of one leg being on the bus and one leg (of the same person that is) off the

m. I put off my pursuit of her for some time, even though I knew I was obliged. I wanted simply to enjoy the office environment without him around for a while. Was that so terrible? Would things really have been so different if I'd started right away?

bus as the bus started moving again. This situation might come about due to the reduced mobility of the geriatric which, in turn related, Marguerite thought, to the first form of fear outlined earlier. Another situation in which this third type of fear was justified by the evidence was one in which, having missed their stop, the pensioner in question has to walk back from the next stop or, if inexplicably a recurrence of the situation occurred, from the one after that or the one after that or the one after that, etc, all the way presumably to the bus depot, exposing them, in their own mind rather than necessarily in reality, to muggings, murder, to a number, in short, of unspeakable – and speakable but unpleasant – things on the walk back to 'their' stop or, rather, back to that place that one presumes is close to their stop and for which reason they had hoped to disembark at that stop, such as their home, their place of worship or their local or a more distant public house.

Marguerite wasn't so concerned about, did not feel, that is, the third kind of fear, which, in fact, as may be clear from the foregoing, he took to be a sub-set of the initial dual variant. Given that it was a bus with an open platform for embarking and disembarking and that he felt relatively fit, he felt the likelihood of sustaining actual physical harm on failing to disembark at the right moment was 'low' or 'very low'. His fear, in short, related more to the risk of exposure, as previously alluded to, a risk that would, he felt, significantly increase were he to be unable to make it to the exit during the window of opportunity when the bus was stationary at the forthcoming stop. And it was for this reason, amongst others, that he resolved, in following the woman in the pinstriped suit, to leave the smallest possible gap between his body and hers without actually touching her, which sweet delight he would reserve for his fleeting moment in passing the conductress, the thought of which made his stomach tingle and flutter slightly. Still, his breathing became more shallow with the realisation that he might miss what he had come to think of unconsciously as 'his' stop, which was not unconnected with the fact that he couldn't set the pace due to the two passengers in front of him, one of which – the female – seemed, remember, to have recognised him.

28

The woman in the pinstriped suit passed something and said something to the conductress as she passed her. Marguerite had been focused, frustratingly, on a different part of the woman's anatomy at the key moment – he had been scrutinising a mole (not the animal) located to one side (the left) on the rear of the woman's neck; this distraction meant that he missed the transaction between the businesswoman, as he assumed her to be, and the conductress, a transaction which, clearly, it would have been most useful for him to have observed. The reasons that it would have been most useful for Marguerite to have observed the transaction between businesswoman and conductress were manifold and included the likelihood that this transaction pertained, in some way, to the disappearance of Harold Absalon who, for those just joining, is or was the Mayor's transport advisor[n] and is or was Marguerite's quarry; another reason why greater vigilance from Marguerite might have been helpful at the crucial moment was that there was a need, in Marguerite's mind, for just such

n. And my work life did start to pick up after he disappeared. Before too long I was reinstated into the monthly meeting, and was actually given part of Harold's brief. At the same time things were unnerving to me, and my situation wasn't helped by this role that he'd thrust upon me regarding his wife.

an object, at this stage, to emerge to help him reinvigorate his investigations.

He had been noticing, as he followed behind the woman in the tight-fitting blue pinstriped suit, the very woman, remember, who had just handed an undisclosed item to the conductress, and said something to her as she passed it and her, that his investigations were at constant risk of going cold, as it was still known as far as he knew, although, again, this depended upon how and when Marguerite's investigations are being apprehended, a question quite beyond his remit, but one which he was dimly aware of. He felt, in short, a constant pressure from his superiors to make progress into the mysterious disappearance of Harold Absalon, and suspected that the handover of an item from woman to woman, the former being dressed, at least (wait for it, wait for it, and don't get excited – it's not that the latter was *un*dressed), as a businesswoman, would somehow relieve some of this perceived pressure. The woman who was dressed, at least (and Marguerite used this formulation once again just to titillate his mind and the minds of anyone who, mysteriously to him, had access to his mind), as a businesswoman had now passed the woman who was dressed, at least (he tried to avoid doing it a third time but failed, telling himself that this would absolutely be the last time) as a bus conductress, the latter being more or less stationary at that point, as has already been indicated, implicitly if not explicitly.

The reason for the formulation 'dressed, at least . . .' in Marguerite's mind may not be apparent to apprentice investigators following, metaphorically speaking, in his footsteps; for that reason he spelt out the reasons why his mind was forming its thoughts in just this way at that moment. The handover of a still undisclosed object by the businesswoman to the conductress without the bidding of the conductress, and the former's words to the latter had, in fact, precipitated Marguerite's use of the formulation 'dressed, at least . . .' since, following and due to this handover, he no longer trusted that the two women in question were businesswoman and conductress, respectively – it had raised the question, in short, as to whether they were businesswoman and conductress or whether they were simply masquerading in those roles in a counter surveillance or even counter insurgency operation, although he had not noticed any original insurgency so to speak, something that he thought he would definitely have noticed even though he had missed the handover from one agent to the other of the item, still undisclosed, in question and the words that had passed between them. The transaction had, in short, put Marguerite on his guard, a guard that had been falling all too easily of late, he noted, especially in relation to what was known in some circles as the fairer sex.

He also noticed, as he approached what he thought of as 'within touching distance' of the conductress, that this progress in his investigations that he felt his superiors demanded had to be of a certain somewhat circumscribed variety – it had to be progress that was at least interesting, preferably suspenseful and, ideally, gripping. That was perhaps just a starting point for defining the type of progress that he felt was demanded of him. There was more that no doubt could be added. Demands were also being placed upon him, he felt, in relation to his investigations, by his peers and by what he momentarily called his inferiors – they were, at least, momentarily, his inferiors in relation to the investigative arts, although through observing his operations they wouldn't, he hoped, be inferior in this relation for ever; it was part of the reason that he had gone into teaching these dark and some lighter arts, that eventually one of his brightest cadets might eclipse the master. The master at that moment, whilst still being vigilant and aware of his surroundings, and being able to smell, he thought, the not unpleasant, lingering fragrance of the woman in the pinstriped suit, tried to bring his mind much more fully back to his investigation into the disappearance of Harold Absalon, the Mayor's transport advisor.

29

He continued to approach the conductress. Was it realistic, he wondered a) that he wouldn't have passed the conductress by now, given the extent of his reflections since the afore- and oft mentioned handover; and b) that he wouldn't have been able to see what the item that had been handed over, so to speak, actually consisted in? He wondered, when eventually presenting this aspect of the case before a jury or a judge or both, whether they would question his mental recording in this regard, along, at the very least, the two-pronged line of questioning that he himself had outlined in the very same mental casebooks? If he were in their shoes he would vigorously pursue the second line of questioning first.

'Why were you unable to see the item in question?' – 'Exhibit J', it might be. Marguerite referred to it as 'Exhibit J' in his mind at this point for a number of reasons, the prime one being that 'Exhibit A' seemed too familiar from the mock trial arena, a secondary reason being that the reference to 'Exhibit J' helpfully served the additional – that is, additional to the useful function of being more plausible and realistic, perhaps more *authentic* might be the word – function of indicating the passage of time within the context of the trial; in other words, whereas 'Exhibit A' would suggest the early stages of a mock or indeed real trial, 'Exhibit J', to Marguerite's mind, was indicative of elapsed judicial time, in the context of that specific trial, whether mock or real. Elapsed judicial time, then, was, he realised now, what he had unconsciously wished to evoke, hence the selection of the letter 'J' as opposed to 'A' in relation to the exhibit in question, namely the unnamed item that the so-called businesswoman had handed to the conductress, a so-called businesswoman whom he thought had recognised him and whom he now thought might be a key lead or even a prime suspect in relation to the disappearance of Harold Absalon, the Mayor's transport advisor.

The fact that Marguerite could imagine, in some future scenario, that the item in question would appear at a trial (etc) in a zip-up or readily closable in some other way plastic sleeve or pocket, did not mean, note, that he could, in this future imagined scenario, see what the item actually was. He was feeling a pressure from an undefined source to somehow reveal what the item in question was, especially as he was now projecting this item forwards into a trial of some sort, and note that this trial, in being referred to as a future event, had taken on more solidity, so to speak, such that Marguerite now felt less at ease in referring to it as a mock rather than a real trial and, for this reason he dispensed in his mind with the term mock in this regard, he refrained, in other words, from referring to that particular trial in that way henceforward. Where was this pressure emanating from, though, he wondered? Was it, as he had thought previously, emerging from his expectation of the expectations of his superiors for what they might refer to as results? He imagined impatience on their parts (and with the emergence of that plural in his mind he now wished that he had referred to 'superior' singular – he felt that in referring to superiors plural that he could, with the emergence of the word 'parts', be accused of pandering to the lewder elements of the jury and he regretted this, since it had not been his intention). They might say to him that he could not make progress in his investigation if he could not identify the item that had been handed to the conductress by the woman whom he was following closely behind. His superior might even pick up on the word 'behind' and its proximity to the word 'parts' as evidence that Marguerite's mind wasn't on the job, with even that final phrase itself emphasising the point.

But underlying this whole issue was an annoyance on Marguerite's part relating to these so-called results, an annoyance that stemmed from a feeling that his superiors, inferiors and peers, anyone, in fact, who had access to these mental notebooks, an access that he now presumed was made possible by their presentation, somehow, at some future real trial, might feel that he was somehow making up the evidence presented at that future trial, that, in short, no actual item had actually changed hands on the top deck of the bus and that, since it was fabricated or, at the very least, doctored or tampered with, that is tampered with or doctored, rather than tampered with or doctored with, which would have a quite different meaning, that he may as well have specified what the item in question actually was. If, as he now imagined with irritation, he was accused, at some future trial, of having fabricated this evidence, that is, of having made up this incident of an item being handed over from an attractive, tightly clad at least in relation to the short pinstriped skirt worn in the usual place, woman to a uniformed conductress, then he left himself open to the charge of laziness in relation to having been bothered to specify what this item was and, further, of lewdness in relation to using this item, reflecting upon it extensively as a means of dwelling much more fully upon the interplay between the two women, each clad seductively, as they were, in their own way, beyond what could plausibly be held up as a realistic timescale, given the external circumstances, which he imagined his interlocutors or interlocutresses would accept as trustworthy for some reason, that is the fact that the woman in question had passed the conductress what seemed like ages before and that it just seemed unlikely, given the fact that Marguerite had been following closely behind the woman, that he would have a) missed what the item actually was and b) had the time, between the woman's passage beyond the conductress and his own, to cogitate so extensively in this way, which is just to recapitulate the two points that had been made earlier, remember, albeit using a somewhat different form of words and presenting the points in reverse order when compared to the previously expressed order. He would stand accused, in short, of both fabrication, imagined fornication and actual indolence, and he couldn't stand that without defending himself in some way.

Why did Marguerite feel he was exposed to this now three-pronged accusation? The reason he intuited this was that he felt that he needed to deliver in some way, and that his interlocutors/-tresses would perhaps do a comparative study between the firmness, the conviction in the telling of the clear and distinct nature of circumstances surrounding being in the position of following behind the woman (or, if you wish, following behind the woman's behind), ie the fact that he was on the top deck of the bus, that the conductress was approaching him etc, with the less than clear, less than distinct object or item passed between the two women. He felt exposed, in short, to an accusation that this sort of item was definitive of what someone in his position as investigator would need in order for judge and jury and, before it got to trial, superiors, peers and inferiors, to be convinced that what was being described was indeed an authentic case; further, that the item, as well as being believable in the context of what could be referred to as the action, might also be of *interest* in some way, might, in short, provide *suspense* in some way as well as a suspension of disbelief, at the very least, if not actual plausibility or veracity. Why, he wondered now, this need for suspense?

30

Marguerite left that question hanging, faced, as he was now, finally, by the conductress. His breathing immediately became shallower at this development and he became what is known as somewhat light-headed. This did not prevent him, professional that he was, from noting that the word 'faced' would imply that the conductress had turned towards him. At least it suggested that she had turned her head towards him, such that the planes of their faces were more or less parallel, give or take a few tens of degrees. In fact, the person who was being faced – Marguerite in the current situation – did not have also to be facing the person who had turned to face them ie the conductress in the current case. Marguerite could, in fact, have had his back to the conductress, as it is known, as she turned to face him, and this would do nothing to undermine her assertion, if she were called as a witness – or suspect even – and was asked, during cross-examination say, whether on such and such a bus travelling along such and such a road at such and such an hour on (etc) day (and the words 'such and such' and 'etc' would almost certainly not be used during the actual questioning; the barrister, attorney or law lord or -lady would insert the actual details as

they understood them, which would probably have been
provided to them by an investigator who, one would hope,
would have been of the calibre of Marguerite although
this, of course, was rare) that she had, indeed, turned to
face him on the bus (etc) in question. What she could not
assert in the circumstance where Marguerite had not been
facing her as she turned to face him and had not turned to
face her for the duration of her facing him was that they
had come what is known as face to face. The meaning of
this term was refreshingly clear, Marguerite thought, as he
scanned the conductress's face for clues as to whether she
would treat him with a modicum of human dignity given
his numerous investigative predicaments. Her expression
was benign, he judged, as he reflected that this term 'face
to face' was what he'd originally had in mind when he'd
used the phrase, in his mind, 'faced as he was now by the
conductress'. A modern variant of the term was 'face time',
as in 'face time with the president'. Personally speaking
he'd never had face time with such luminaries as presi-
dents or even ministers, whether prime or otherwise – the
minister that is – whether of his own, so to speak, country
or continent or another country or continent, although he
felt sure that if he was successful in uncovering the circumstances surrounding the disappearance of Harold
Absalon, the Mayor's transport advisor don't forget, and
even managed to find the man himself, that is Harold[o]

o. It was around this time, then, that my colleagues started calling me
'Harold'. I was unsettled by it, to start with, but I could see, over time, that
my own surprise at being called 'Harold' was making my colleagues uneasy.
So after a while, I just adopted it. I even took on some of his mannerisms
and phraseologies. That seemed to settle the atmosphere somewhat, at least
for a time.

Absalon, the Mayor's transport advisor, then the president, minister of whatever stature or even the Queen herself would seek an audience with him (Marguerite), one that he thought he would be all too willing to give (if this is what one did, ie *give* an audience), at the Monarch's, Minister's or President's earliest convenience, their schedule likely as it was, to be fuller at that stage, given the wrapping up, as it might be known, of the case of the disappearance of Harold[p] Absalon, given, in fact, that their schedules were almost certainly fuller most of the time than Marguerite's despite the incredible assiduousness of his approach to his investigations.

The conductress had turned to face him, as has already been established beyond reasonable doubt. Further, they were, finally, face to face, which implied that Marguerite had either been facing the conductress, that is, after she had turned to face him and before she turned away from him, assuming that she would, or that he had turned to face her within the parameters, as previously established, of her facing him. This did *not* mean, as far as Marguerite was concerned, that their current face-to-face constituted 'face time' as he thought of it. If, as was possible, the bus conductress became Justice Minister, Minister of Transport, say, President or – and this was even less plausible, the 'even' indicating succinctly and skilfully that the first three outcomes were themselves quite unlikely to obtain – the Queen (and he didn't entertain the idea of her becoming the King, given the already high levels of implausibility

p. I saw, in short, how much potential there was in my taking on his persona in terms of advancing my career. That's why I started doing it, even though I have to say I've never felt entirely comfortable with it.

of options under consideration) then Marguerite would accept that their time spent face to face in this scenario following his solving of a particularly intractable future case, might then constitute face time; similarly if he found that he became President etc (and presumably he would know to some extent that this was happening to him, in advance, that is, of him taking office as it was known – he couldn't imagine that the presidency (etc) would be conferred upon him without his prior knowledge or consent), then the conductress might conceivably seek an audience with *him*, which, given his current interest in her, he thought he would be minded to grant, in which case, when it occurred, she could justifiably refer to it as face time with him, if she so wished. For now, she held his gaze and he held hers. She had such dark brown eyes – both of them – to the extent that he could almost not distinguish the pupils from the irises. After a very short time had elapsed in this way she looked down into her right hand, the one into which the woman in front of Marguerite had placed something. Marguerite also looked down to the same location. The hand contained a number of coins which, as far as Marguerite could make out were genuine; that is they were not counterfeit; further, they were of the currency, as far as he could tell from his vantage point two or three feet above them, that pertained to the land he inhabited – that is the physical rather than necessarily the mental space in which he resided. The conductress put the coins in her low-slung leather money belt, reached into a separate compartment of the money belt and handed Marguerite two coins of a smaller denomination but which nevertheless also seemed genuine and relevant, currency-wise, to his current physical context. In this way Marguerite assuaged his disappointment at not having had the opportunity of squeezing past the conductress, or even brushing up against her, something that he felt was somehow now inappropriate given that they had, so recently, been face to face or near face to face in the way described (although note that face time, interestingly, did not, to Marguerite's mind, preclude such squeezing or brushing up against, although he personally would not abuse his position in that way, he thought, should he find himself in that situation).

A question emerged, then: why had the woman he was following behind paid his bus fare?

31

This action on the part of the woman in the pinstriped suit – namely that of her paying his bus fare – had the effect of making Marguerite review his operational parameters in relation to her. Hitherto, note, he had simply been following *behind* her; now, he made the snap operational decision to actively *follow* her.

Was he being rash, he wondered, as he followed her towards the rear of the bus, in so decisively deleting the word 'behind' to simply leave the word 'following' within his mission parameters in relation to the woman in the pinstriped suit? Some might accuse him of starting to follow her on a whim, as a result of her small act of kindness towards him in paying his fare. Others might say that he had changed his mission parameters simply on the basis of animal instinct related to the scent that she gave off, whether this scent had been applied by her or had arisen naturally, as it were, from her body, or an admixture of the two, a scent that had only recently entered Marguerite's nasal passages and fired the neural networks associated therewith. Perhaps the kindness and the attraction had combined, resulting in the unceremonious ditching of his previous parameters; that is, perhaps his unprofessional affections had alighted on this woman *precisely because of* the kindness she had shown towards him. Still others may accuse him of starting to follow the woman on a different type of whim, that is, a non-sexual one and one unmoved by the kindness that she had so recently shown towards him: perhaps he had simply become bored following passively behind her and had wanted to take a more active role in his investigation and had, on this basis, swiftly decided to start following her, this decision coincidentally taking place shortly after she had paid his bus fare. Was it that he had started to feel like a victim of circumstance rather than an active agent in the investigation of the missing transport advisor?

Having so summarily and decisively changed his mission parameters in the manner described, he now, equally summarily and decisively, dismissed all those who held that he had done so on a whim. He dismissed all those who would assert that the speed with which he had decided to follow this woman was indicative of a descent down the food chain from the summits of clarity, probity (in a specific sense) and professionalism for which he was rightly, to his mind, renowned. Similarly, he dismissed from his mind those who would hold that his boredom or otherwise was relevant in some way – he might find himself bored by a particular clue relating to Harold Absalon's disappearance but this would certainly not mean that he would dismiss such a clue, just as he would not follow something up simply because it was of interest, whether sexually or otherwise, to him, if it did not pertain to the investigation that he was engaged in, an investigation that remained unchanged, remember, despite his hasty change in mission parameters. Nor was the speed with which he had made the original decision indicative of the random drifting of his mind from one object – Isobel Absalon, say – to another, the woman in the tight-fitting pinstriped suit, say. He felt that he had established beyond reasonable doubt that his mind did not drift randomly in this way but moved magisterially from one tightly argued and justified arena to another as he remorselessly narrowed in on the circumstances surrounding the disappearance (etc). It was this ability to review his mission parameters, on the spot, within a split second or so, even when he was in what was known in the manuals as a tight spot, that set Marguerite apart from other investigators. The speed with which he changed from following behind to following the woman in question was a distillation of his years of training and experience into a moment that looked instinctive, a moment in which he trusted wholeheartedly that he had made the right decision despite the dangers potentially arising from that decision, dangers that did not, in other words, pertain just to the speed with which the decision had been made but to the content of the decision itself, that is, the dangers inherent in deciding to follow the woman in question who, remember, seemed to have recognised him, instead of simply following behind her. The decision, then, was surely a lesson to all budding detectives who, through whatever means, had managed to observe his mind changing so rapidly in relation to his mission parameters if not in relation to his ultimate objective, which remained unchanged from wishing to unearth, if he could express it in that way, the circumstances surrounding, so to speak, the disappearance of Harold Absalon, the Mayor's transport advisor.

32

By the time Marguerite's transaction with the conductress had been concluded, and his nuanced distinctions
between following and following behind had been made,
the woman in the pinstriped suit was very nearly upon the
stairs at the rear of the bus. The man in front of her, who
had, of course, not been the subject of Marguerite's most
recent reflections, had paused at the top of those stairs
which, to Marguerite's mind, could only mean one thing:
that someone was traversing those very stairs in the opposite direction; that is, that person was *as*cending (no pun
intended), thereby blocking the passage of those, such as
the gentleman, the woman in the pinstriped suit and Marguerite himself, who wished to descend. That, at least, was
Marguerite's snap analysis of the situation once he had
looked far enough ahead of the pinstriped woman's rear
end to see the man in front poised, somewhat impatiently
it would seem, at the top of the stairs. How Marguerite
was able to judge of the man's impatience even though he
could not see his face – the seat, if we can call it that, ordinarily, of the outward expression of emotion – he would
leave to others to fathom. He stayed focused, instead, on
the tableau that had presented itself to his visual (and no

doubt to his sixth, that is his sleuth's) sense which, to reiterate, was the momentary pause between the man's arrival at the top of the curved flight of stairs at the rear of the bus and the commencement of his descent, a pause that edged its way almost imperceptibly, with each word of Marguerite's thoughts, towards a proper interval of time, from a lull, interval, short while or juncture, perhaps, to anything up to an age, epoch or eternity. The fact that the man was still waiting there at the exhaustion of this list in Marguerite's mind should not be taken to imply that the man had been waiting for the length of time indicated by the final item in the list; rather it should be taken as indicative of the startling speed with which Marguerite was able to appraise himself of a situation, this despite the pressure that he felt to deliver results in the case of the disappearance of Harold Absalon[q].

Some may be wondering why it had taken so long, in fact, for Marguerite to notice again the man in front of the woman in the pinstriped suit. Certainly (and he would refer back in his thinking if he could) the man in front, so to speak, had not been part of his deliberations for some time, so focused had he been on the woman in the pinstriped suit and, more specifically, on the rear end of that woman, in its closely tailored pinstriped skirt and, more importantly in relation to the disappearance of Harold Absalon, the triangulated transaction, as he now thought of it, between her, the bus conductress and himself, which had resulted in his

q. My confidence returned. I felt able to hold my own in the monthly meeting, perhaps for the first time. Granted, people did start to look at me somewhat askance, as though they suspected I was somehow implicated. But no-one voiced anything directly to me. And some of those who had shunned me whilst he'd been around actually started laughing at my jokes.

bus fare being paid. Some may think, somewhat cynically, that the re-emergence of the man was rather convenient, that without some progress along the top deck by one of the triumvirate of Marguerite, the woman (as before) and the man (again, as before) then Marguerite might find himself atop the top deck almost indefinitely. The cynics, in other words, might accuse Marguerite of conveniently remembering the man in question to get himself out of a hole or, more specifically given the genre and tradition that he was thinking in, the tight spot that he found himself in atop that bus. To be even more explicit and blatantly accusatory – and don't forget that this is all just the unfolding of Marguerite's own mind, his lower self accusing his higher self perhaps, whatever that means – that his investigation had been going nowhere until this man had reappeared in Marguerite's consciousness, helpfully and he hoped suspensefully drawing attention to the top step, at least to the general vicinity of the stairs and the expectation that someone of central importance to Marguerite's investigation into the disappearance of Harold Absalom might imminently appear (someone like Isobel Absalom, you say? – it's possible), thereby enabling Marguerite to retain the attention of his funders and followers, such as your good self. After all, he needed to be funded somehow, the few coins that he now had in his possession only taking him so far; he was conscious, then, of needing to give his faithful subscribers what was known in some circles as value for money; he had confidence in his own investigative abilities, that much was apparent; however, he was conscious that he must also keep his subscribers informed of progress, otherwise they might withdraw their subscription. He did not begrudge doing this and he wasn't just saying *this* to keep his subscribers on side. Without them, in short, his investigation would not have got off the ground in the first place. He was conscious, in short, of the need to demonstrate the progress that he was making in his investigation and that, to some – whether they be subscribers *or* borrowers – it would seem that his investigation had entered into a zone of stasis, incapable perhaps of moving meaningfully forwards. He wanted to assuage those doubts, keep those doubters on-side and he knew that the emergence of a vital clue or, were what he was engaged in to be fictional, which of course it is not, a startling twist in the plot, would go some way to doing this – how could a sleuth of his acuity not know this? What he was denying – and he was willing, if called upon, to do so under oath – was that he had engineered the situation in his mind so that the gentleman suddenly, after so much slow-moving action (according to some reviewers) attained the top of the stairs and had to wait there, pregnantly (using that term metaphorically) whilst someone (or some thing?) moved up the stairway towards him, soon to appear in Marguerite's perception of the scene. What he was denying, then, was fabricating this scene – or any of the scenes so far witnessed by him – as a means of keeping his investigation into the disappearance of the Mayor's transport advisor alive.

He reflected that the term 'cliff-hanger' had presumably been coined to evoke the situation in which a person, following a dramatic set of circumstances, plot twists and other devices on the part of the producer, writer and/or director, finds themselves hanging from a cliff either: a) from a conveniently placed shrub, bush or other tenuously attached item of vegetation, or b) from the eroding cliff-edge by their fingernails, the toenails not really lending themselves dramatically in the same way, except perhaps in the case of our simian cousins whom we can and do care for to some extent but not to the extent of a fully human human perhaps, especially when said fully human human happens to fall into the somewhat ill-defined category, to Marguerite's mind, of 'damsel' about which more, perhaps, later.

So much for the origins of the terminology. What of the accusation of him engineering such a cliff-hanger by placing the man at the top of the stairs – his cliff, so to speak – and making him wait there? In short he would unequivocally and unreservedly deny that this was what he had done, assuming he had the capacity to see that this was what had been needed at that moment and that he was able to fulfil this requirement, which he also denied. Quite simply he had noticed the man in front of the woman in the pinstriped suit again as a result of the geometry of the upper deck: he had been taking a professional and, he admitted it, personal interest in said woman – especially in her rear end, so to speak – and this meant that there was but a short distance between him and her to the extent that her body, so much the focus of his attentions, had served to obscure what was in front of it further down the aisle. This situation had suddenly and dramatically changed when the gentleman had moved onto the landing at the top of the stairs, which happened to be to the left of the aisle and the woman within it, from Marguerite's perspective, and had thereby come, as it were, once again, into Marguerite's purview. Granted there was nothing to prevent the man from having been within Marguerite's mind up until that point ie within the purview of his imagination. That he did not appear in this way expresses something of the assiduousness with which Marguerite had been pursuing, more recently, in all senses of the word that he could think of, the woman in the pinstriped suit. In other words it was the reappearance, given the geometry of the top deck, and other circumstances too numerous to enter into, of the gentleman in actuality rather than in his imagination that had triggered Marguerite's reflections on the cliff-hanger ending of episodes: he had not imaginatively *put* the man there waiting pregnantly (etc) at the top of the stairs so as to *bring about* such a cliff-hanger, knowing in a way difficult to ascribe to him, that such a cliff-hanger would be most timely. It may seem too convenient but who can deny the firm analytic foundation given by Marguerite relating to the geometry of the situation?

Marguerite's accusers may accuse him further of protesting his innocence a mite too vociferously. Further, they might, he imagined, accuse him of desperation in his appeal to geometry as the firm foundation for what he claimed was unfolding on the top deck of the bus. Finally, at least for now, they might accuse him of implausibility in glimpsing the blonde shock[r] of Isobel Absalom's hair momentarily at the top step, as he did at that very moment.

r. Once I'd reestablished my career, *then* I started following her. And once I started following her, I went at it like a maniac, couldn't help myself.

It disappeared almost as soon as it had appeared, leaving the gentleman to commence his descent and leaving Marguerite questioning the veracity of his initial identification of a momentary flash of brightness as the person of Harold Absalom's wife. After all, if she was pursuing him then what had precipitated her immediate retreat? Had the woman in the pinstriped suit signalled to her in some way? Or was it simply the knowledge that Marguerite would soon be passing down those very stairs? All would be revealed in the next episode, perhaps.

33

Fixated, as he had been, momentarily, by the flash of brightness that had appeared at the top of the stairs, Marguerite had failed to notice something that was perhaps even more troubling to him: another double decker bus had appeared in the rear window of the bus that they were travelling upon. Not only had it appeared, but it appeared, momentarily, to be about to career, as it is known for some reason, into the back of the bus that they were travelling upon. Furthermore, there were three passengers at the front of the top deck of this second bus who had clocked, as it was known, Marguerite's imminent, now, disembarkation and who were making ready to disembark themselves so as, he suspected, to apprehend or otherwise prevent him from continuing his investigation into the disappearance of Harold Absalon, the Mayor's transport advisor. Such was the situation as it was unfolding on the ground, so to speak.

The apparent imminent collision between the two large passenger vehicles did not deter Marguerite from reflecting in a measured, calm and clear way, as was his wont, on the circumstances surrounding the recent acquisition of this second bus within what he thought of at that moment as his sense domain. To express it more simply, as those cross-examining him would no doubt duly ask him to do in the courts, why was it only then that he noticed this second bus in his field of vision? Surely, given his standing posture – indeed, given his walking vantage point atop the bus – he would have had a reasonably clear view of any trailing bus prior to the moment of descension, if that is the word, by the gentleman that they were following behind, *despite* the distracting flash of brightness at the top of the stairs. Or was Marguerite to make the same move as he had most recently made in relation to that gentleman by contending that all of his attention had hitherto been focused on the woman in the pinstriped suit whom, lately, he had taken to including in the plural personal pronoun 'they', to the exclusion of all others, as though their relationship had suddenly developed intimately? Marguerite's response to this irritatingly persistent line of questioning would, he thought, be fourfold: i). yes, it was true that initially the allure of the woman in the pinstriped suit had been such that it had sucked, so to speak, all of his attention towards her to the extent that, even though he was taller than she was, which meant that if he held himself fully erect, he might, in theory, if he'd so wished and if he'd had his sur-veillance wits about him, so to speak, have been able to peer above her head and out of the rear window of the bus to see the second bus still in the distance, comparatively, but there none the less and gaining on the bus that they were currently travelling upon; but he had decided not to peer, fully erect, above her head in the manner described. That accounted, in Marguerite's mind, for part of his journey along the aisle. ii). Secondly (as has already been indicated by the Roman numerals) and most importantly, to Marguerite's mind, was that the gentleman who was continuing to descend, as far as Marguerite could tell, step by step towards the lower deck, happened, as it happens, to be a tall, upright fellow. In other words, that was this man's general disposition; Marguerite could, when the mood took him or when required for operational reasons, make himself erect, as referred to in i. but it was not his general physiological demeanour, so to speak, whereas with this fellow it was. His observations of the fellow were, Marguerite conceded, somewhat contrary to the training that he had received in this area at cadet school, which indicated that tall people tended to stoop rather like an apology for their increased height in relation to most of the remaining populace. That was just a guide, of course, and when in the field it was imperative to amend one's views based on the circumstances that actually presented themselves. In this case, one of the circumstances was that despite being quite tall, but not to the extent of having to duck to pass along the aisle on the top deck of the bus, and broad-shouldered, but not to the extent that he needed to pass sideways down said aisle, the gentleman that they'd been following behind and continued to follow behind, was not apologetic about his height or width (his girth, note, was about standard given his height and width, Marguerite had judged, as best he could, from the rear, so to speak). That is to say that his general demeanour was not one of apology, nor did he more vocally express his condolences to his fellow passengers for the somewhat larger space that he inhabited compared to most if not all of them. The point that Marguerite was quite plausibly making here was that, given the fact that the man was taller and wider than Marguerite, that it was not until the man had vacated the aisle, a word that takes on a somewhat different connotation now that Marguerite had started referring rather familiarly to himself and the woman (etc, as before) as 'they' or, if he were to be addressed directly about it, which was not possible in the circumstances, as 'we', that Marguerite had not been able to see the full extent of the rear window of the bus – the height, specifically and, to a lesser extent, the width of the man in front of him had prevented him from being able to see the central section of that window. It was only now, with the man off to one side continuing to descend before his eventual disembarkation that, taking his eyes off the shorter, narrower, but much more enticing frame of the woman in the you-know-what, and no longer being distracted by any flashes at the top of the stairs, Marguerite was able to take in the full extent of what was taking place behind the bus, which was that another bus looked, still, as though it was going to career into it, that is, into the bus that they, to put it cosily once again, were travelling upon. This was not to say that the man was wider than the bus. Of course not. It was all a question of perspective.

To continue upon the fourfold root of his inability to see the pressing nature of the bus following them: iii). Such perspective meant that, even were this upright, tall and wide gent to have been in place further along the aisle, in front, that is, of the woman in the pinstriped suit, that given the proximity, now, of the bus behind the one they were travelling upon, Marguerite *would* have been able to see this following bus, given that that bus now much more fully occupied the visual space afforded by the window at the rear of the top deck of the bus, a window that Marguerite continued to approach despite this looming within it of the trailing, but rapidly gaining, bus. In still other words, the upright man, when Marguerite and the woman had been following him along the aisle, had only hidden the central portion of the rear window, leaving the window's extremities exposed. Had there been anything extreme to observe through these exposed areas then Marguerite would have observed and duly reported it.

iv).ly, and finally, this being a fourfold defence of his actions in that split second between glimpsing what he thought was Isobel Absalon's still quite newly bleached hair[s] and glancing over the head of the woman he was following to see, through the rear window, the double decker bus bearing down on them, was a more hypothetical analysis of whether, even if he'd had a clear view through the rear window, he'd have been able to see the other double decker bus. His reasoning ran quite straightforwardly as follows. It may have been that the rear window was too low down, given the relative positions of the two buses, to see the rear bus until it was nearly upon them, especially in the case where a valley was involved and the front bus, if it can be referred to in that way, which clearly it can be, were to be moving uphill, as it is known, with the rear bus still moving downhill, as it is known, behind it, having not yet

---

s. Why was I eventually so zealous in my pursuit of her? Now that my career was back on track, I *wanted* her, quite simply, along with the rest of Harold's lifestyle, and I thought that any dirt I could find on her would help successfully to bring that about.

reached the valley's nadir, as it were. In that situation not only the valley itself but also the rear of the front bus could obscure the rear bus: all that would be viewable through the rear window might be the road surface with its various markings, say, or a man or woman on a bike behind the first bus. Even in the absence of the valley, whether shallow or quite deep, it might have been that the rear window was placed at such a lowly position in relation to the rear bus that the latter would not in any case have been visible from the upper deck of the former until the latter was virtually upon the former, as with the preceding three circumstances. However, given that the previous three conditions did in fact pertain, namely and in summary that Marguerite had been focusing on the woman in the pinstriped suit and then on what he took to be Isobel Absalon at the critical moments, that the man was partially in the way of the rear window and that the bus had still been sufficiently distant to be completely obscured by the man, then Marguerite could not judge whether the fourth condition pertained, except to say that there was no valley involved in the scenario on the ground, as it were, and that the actual window was indeed quite low down in the rear of the top deck of the bus. Neither could he reconstruct the necessary circumstances at that moment, given that the trailing bus now *completely* filled the rear view from the top deck, hence Marguerite's insistence on the word 'hypothetical' in relation to this final condition.

At that moment the bus that they were travelling upon came to an abrupt halt, as it is known, as, much to his relief, did the bus behind it, just a few inches separating them at rest. He had a clear view of those standing up on the top deck prior to disembarkation from the latter now and, even though a collision had been averted, his mind had not been put to rest regarding the collection of unsavouries (which, as before, was not to say that they were sweet) standing up on the top deck in preparation, he assumed, to exit that bus, a number of whom, he was sure, earpieces in ears, had clocked, as it was known, his own imminent disembarkation. It made the next few moments in Marguerite's pursuit of Harold Absalon, the Mayor's transport advisor, perilous indeed.

34

Marguerite noticed that the agents on the other bus had only started moving once his way was clear to see them, sight, in his experience, generally being a reciprocal arrangement; that is, to his mind, him seeing them implied that they had also seen *him*; they had seen him, more-over, attempting to disembark; and it was this, Marguerite thought, that had precipitated their action against him.

Outwardly he gave nothing away, as it were – not even a flicker of recognition: his pursuers knowing that he had seen them would have made shaking them off even more problematical. The reason that his pursuers knowing that he'd seen them would have made shaking them off even more problematical related to the fact that whilst the pursuer remained undetected[t], to that extent they had what was known as 'the upper hand', meaning that they were in the driving seat, so to speak, as far as the pursuit was concerned. Now the same applied to the pursued: to the extent that they could maintain a facade, at least, that they had not noticed that they were being pursued, then, to that

t. After a while, I managed to enter the marital home. I used every device and undercover gizmo I could lay my hands on to track her. I put cameras in the bedrooms, and at other places she frequented. I left, as they say, no stone unturned.

extent, they would have the upper hand unless, of course, the pursuer knew that the pursued had noticed them, despite the pursued's best efforts in terms of restraining changes in facial expressions, mainly, in which case the pursuer would maintain the upper hand provided they, in turn, did not volunteer any facial expression or any other indication to the pursued that they, the pursuer, knew that the pursued knew that they were being pursued, that the pursued, in short, knew that they could refer to themselves, at that moment, as 'pursued'. Of course if the pursuer and pursued were both aware of each other (and the pursuer couldn't fail to be aware of the pursued of course; were he, or exceptionally she, not aware then the whole situation would fall down) and were both aware that their counter-part – that is the pursuer in the case of the pursued and the pursued in the case of the pursuer (and the latter could, of course, have been more succinctly expressed, or thought, by Marguerite, as 'vice versa') – was aware of them, that is the pursuer was aware that the pursued was aware that the pursuer was pursuing them and the pursued was aware that the pursuer was aware that the pursued knew that the pursuer was pursuing them, then no-one had the upper hand, which meant, by logical extension, that no-one had the lower hand either. The situation that pertained, as Marguerite continued to move towards the stairs, was one in which, to the best of his knowledge, as it was often referred to, he thought, given all of his experience, that he would not have vouchsafed to his pursuers that he knew that they were pursuing him; equally, though, if they had done their research on him then they would know that, given his level of experience of such pursuits, he would be unlikely to vouchsafe such knowledge in such a situation, in which case them merely clocking him clocking them as he had done through the rear window of the bus upon which he was travelling without, of course, showing outwardly that he knew that they were pursuing him, would have been sufficient for them, if they had their wits about them, to know that he knew that they were pursuing him, in which case neither of them had the upper or, as before, the lower hand as was the case in the previous scenario and, as before, neither was in the driver's seat nor, by extension, in the passenger seat. In short, then, Marguerite judged that he could not simply give them the slip on the basis that they didn't know that he knew that they were pursuing him – he assumed that they did in fact know that he knew that they were pursuing him. He had to pit what he took to be his superior knowledge of pursuits in general, then, against what he took, by implication, to be their inferior knowledge of such pursuits to shake them off in the full knowledge by both parties that a pursuit was taking place at that moment and that both parties were involved in that pursuit. That was the situation Marguerite found himself in as he continued to approach the stairs at the rear of the top deck of the bus, with all of the potential threats that they entailed.

35

Marguerite had not failed to notice that the bus upon which his pursuers were travelling was a much newer model than the bus upon which he was travelling. This was no idle observation. In fact, none of Marguerite's observations was idle, to his mind. How, though, was it germane to his investigation that the pursuing bus was a newer model than the bus upon which he was travelling? Well, in this way: it made the starting positions for him and for his pursuers more evenly matched. Marguerite knew, essentially, that on the more modern buses, such as the one that his pursuers had travelled upon, the stairs were located towards the middle or front of the vehicle, whereas on the bus upon which he was travelling, the stairs were located towards the rear of the vehicle, as has long been established. This was germane, then, since, were the stairs on the pursuing vehicle to have been at the rear, were it, in other words, to have been of the same, or similar, make and model as the bus that Marguerite was travelling upon, then this would have given Marguerite an extra few seconds in which to make his escape, an escape, that is, back undercover, from where he could operate much more effectively in unearthing the circumstances surrounding the disappearance of Harold Absalon, the Mayor's transport advisor.

Despite this relative disadvantage on Marguerite's part in relation to bus exit points, he deduced that the risk of his pursuers storming the top deck of the bus that he was travelling upon was still low, given that the stairwell was blocked – partially, but sufficiently to Marguerite's mind – by the gentleman who was slowly using it, together with the handrail, to descend to the lower deck. This meant that it would be difficult for anyone to ascend at that moment; certainly it would be difficult for a number of people to ascend at speed, as would probably need to be the case for those people to be effective in apprehending Marguerite, the speed being required in order to take Marguerite by surprise, something that happened rarely, and the crowd scene, as it was known, being required to overwhelm him physically, given that his close-contact, hand-to-hand combat skills were likely to be far too dextrous and crafty for any single individual, whether male or female, to deal with.

He had established in his mind, then, that his pursuers, were there any, would have to wait for his descent at least to the lower deck and probably to the pavement or sidewalk, in order to try to apprehend him – this is what the gentleman and, imminently now, the woman in the pinstriped suit had achieved and were achieving for him in preceding him in descending the curved flight of stairs at the rear of the bus. In short, they were buying him time.

He didn't need much time, however, to ascertain that what he needed was much more time than the gentleman and the woman in pinstriped suit would provide for him. It wasn't as though his pursuers would be thwarted simply by having to wait a few extra seconds for Marguerite to emerge rather than being able to storm the upper deck as they might have hoped to do. It was not as though they would simply lose interest in the pursuit in those few elapsed seconds or fractions of seconds. What, then, would the additional time bought for him, in effect, by the gentleman and the woman in the pinstriped suit, mean for him in terms of eluding his pursuers whilst attempting, of course, to continue to follow the woman in the pinstriped suit? How, in other words, could he most usefully use the time generously bought or inadvertently bequeathed to him by the gentleman and the woman in the pinstriped suit?

The additional time would crucially allow him to create what is known as a diversion. This *would*, he judged, buy him sufficient time to elude his pursuers. In other words, time being money, he would invest the time bought for or bequeathed to him, by the aforementioned people, in a diversion that would give him sufficient time to give his pursuers the slip, as it is known. And, looking at the backs of the legs of the woman in the pinstriped suit as she continued towards the stairs, he knew just the sort of diversion that he would need.

36

Marguerite's inquiries had established, beyond reasonable doubt, that the bus that he was travelling upon had already stopped. Regardless of whether it had stopped at an official stop or not, this afforded the woman in the pinstriped suit the opportunity of disembarking, and, as she started down the stairs, she seemed eager not to miss that opportunity. Indeed she might be aware, in a way that Marguerite was not, that the bus had *not* stopped at an official stop, in which case her window of opportunity might be smaller than if it had stopped at an official stop. The reason for this was that the driver, whether male or female, was not obliged to wait at this unofficial stop until all of the passengers who wanted to leave the bus had left the bus and all of the potential passengers who wanted to join the bus had joined the bus. Essentially, in this situation of alighting from or embarking upon the bus away from an official (etc) stop, regardless of whether the bus was stationary or in motion, one 'took one's chances', as it was known. The bus driver might pause out of kindness and consideration, having seen you moving left to right or right to left in his mirror, but this wouldn't go on indefinitely.

This contrasted with the official stop, where the driver

was obliged to wait until everyone who wanted to exit the bus had exited and all those who wanted to enter the bus had entered. Well, as so often, it wasn't quite as simple as that, Marguerite reflected, as he watched the woman in the pinstriped suit descending the stairs and prepared to follow suit (no pun intended). In order to stand a good chance of entering the bus, you had to be at, or close to, the bus stop and you, or someone who fulfilled the condition of being at or close to the bus stop, must signal successfully to the driver that you wanted him or her to stop. Marguerite had often seen people racing to the stop, on foot this generally was, with the bus already stopped and the last passengers having already boarded the bus; the bus driver was not obliged to wait for these tardy sprinters, although he may choose to do so if he was of that mien, or if he was of that mien on that particular day, or at that particular hour or minute of that particular day. Similarly, the driver was not obliged to wait indefinitely at the bus stop if someone had pushed the button, if it was a button, or pulled the cord (etc) if that latter situation pertained, but had not disembarked for whatever reason, as might be the case with the woman in the pinstriped suit, hence, perhaps, her haste. Similarly in the case where the person wishing to disembark had not pushed the button or pulled the cord, on which situation pertained, but had relied upon the fact that another person had pushed the button or pulled the cord, regardless of whether they were acquainted with that person or related to them or whatever, in which case they would only push or pull the button or cord respectively for emphasis which, in the situation under examination was hardly ever necessary. It was this latter situation, then, that pertained to Marguerite and the woman in the pinstriped suit, namely, the cord, in this case, had been pulled, ringing the bell both in the driver's cab and on both the lower and upper deck, since if the bell only rang in the driver's cab then each passenger wishing to disembark would have to ring it; at least each passenger wishing to disembark who had not *seen* another passenger pulling the cord, sticking with the current scenario, in advance of the stop that they wanted, but not so far in advance that it was also before the stop before the one that they wanted, would have themselves to pull the cord and this would inevitably lead, to Marguerite's mind, more often than not, to more than one bell ring in the driver's cab when one bell ring would more often than not suffice. That was why the system was rigged up so that when anyone (excluding the driver, note, at least when he was in his cab) pulled the cord then everyone else on the bus, including the driver this time, would hear it provided that they had suitable auditory apparatus and that other sounds were relatively quiet at the moment that the bell in question rang.

The bell had rung, then, a little while earlier and the woman in the pinstriped suit was eager, it would appear, to disembark at this stop, which was, Marguerite was sure, a so-called official stop and one, moreover, that the woman in the pinstriped suit seemingly identified as her own, as it were. In fact she needn't have worried, to Marguerite's mind, because it was the job of the conductor or conductress on the type of open-platformed buses on which they (as before) were travelling to indicate to the driver, whether male or female, that they – the driver – could set off again from the stop. The reason that it was the job of the conductress, to bring it back to the current actual situation again, was that she was more at liberty than the driver to check that all of the passengers that wanted to disembark had indeed disembarked and also that all those who wanted and were able to board had indeed done so. She was more at liberty to check this because she could walk around the bus from top to bottom, checking whether everyone who wanted to had exited or entered. The driver was generally stuck in his cab, at least whilst he was driving (and Marguerite included waiting at a bus stop, engine running, under the rubric of 'driving') and, whilst he had a number of mirrors, these contained blind spots within which passengers waiting to disembark at the last minute could lurk. Thus the bus authorities had devised the ingenious team-working system whereby the conductress was the eyes of the driver whilst the bus was stationary at a bus stop and she would indicate the all-clear, that is that everyone had exited or entered who wanted to exit or enter, within the confines of time and space alluded to above, by pulling the cord, or pressing the button, twice, note, and this double push served to differentiate it from the single push of the passenger; indeed it was only the conductress who was allowed to execute the double push – this was part of the authority vested in her, alongside her revenue collection and other functions. And indeed the conductress was now right behind Marguerite, who wanted to point this out to the woman in the pinstriped suit. He wanted to explain to the woman in the pinstriped suit, now that she had moved so hastily away from him, that she needn't have worried about missing her stop – the bus would not be moving again until the conductress had done the double push, if we can call it that, and she wouldn't be in a position to do that, Marguerite thought, until both he and the woman in the pinstriped suit had in any case exited the bus, for the simple reason that the conductress would need to move down to the bottom deck before undertaking the double push, to ensure that all of the passengers and potential passengers who wanted to travel on that bus at that particular moment, within the confines outlined above, had safely got onto the bus, and she would have to wait for Marguerite and the woman in the pinstriped suit to at least descend the stairs before she could do this, thereby giving them ample time, in Marguerite's estimation, to exit the bus. What Marguerite did next, however, changed this situation somewhat: he stood to one side of the top step; more specifically he stood to the right hand side of the top step to allow the conductress to move in front of him and down the stairs, which she duly did, without brushing past him, alas, and with just the faintest of quizzical looks in his direction.

37

Having waited a few moments for the conductress to descend a number of stairs, Marguerite reached up and swiftly double-pressed the button on the rear wall of the top deck of the bus. The bus immediately lurched forwards, causing the conductress and a number (unspecified) of passengers on the lower deck, or on their way to the lower deck, to exclaim in a variety of ways, one emitting an abrupt scream, another saying 'Oi!', and also there was a bark, surprisingly enough.

Notice that Marguerite had waited a few moments before double-pressing the button. What were his intentions in pausing in this way? What were his intentions more widely? In asking those two questions of himself, as he quickly moved away from the vicinity of the button and towards the stairs again with the aid of a vertical handrail located immediately to the right of the top step, Marguerite was aware that the answers were related. In fact, it could be said that a single answer might suffice to answer both questions and, indeed, the following, tertiary, question: what was that answer? The answer to the three questions was that he wanted the curved stairway to be clear or clearing to allow him to alight from the bus, an act he wished to engage in whilst, note, the bus was in motion. He was unhappy with how he had formulated this answer in his mind, and he immediately attempted to reformulate it. He had paused to ensure that it was simpler for the people who had hitherto occupied the stairway to vacate that stairway by continuing to descend, thereby allowing him to alight. No, that did not quite do it either, he realised, as he took the first step down the stairway. In attempting to answer the three questions succinctly for the third time, he would focus, as he very much enjoyed doing, on the conductress and her role in the affair of the double-pressing, as he now came to think of it. He had paused to allow the conductress to pass the half-way down mark on the curved stairway at the rear of the bus – not that there was an actual mark of course. The purpose of the pause, then, was to attempt to ensure that it was easier for the conductress to continue to descend rather than to turn around on the stairs and start ascending towards him, thereby preventing his own descent and eventual alighting from the bus. But he hadn't wanted to pause for too long, since this might have meant that the conductress may, by that time, have attained, so to speak, the lower deck and might have been reaching up herself to the button for her own official, as it were, double-press, which would have put Marguerite in a difficult position, he judged, since it might have enabled his pursuers from the top deck of the other bus to have alighted from that bus and to have boarded the bus that he was on – to have joined, in short, Isobel Absalon[u] on the bottom deck,

u. I would stay up through the night sometimes, analysing tapes, trying to place the faces around her. That's when the key strand – or shard, I should say – of evidence came into my hands. That's when I knew I was really onto something.

assuming that she was there, meaning that his own options for alighting and eluding them would have been substantially diminished. He didn't want that. He wanted to remain 'at large', as it was known, for as long as possible. Tempted, as he was, by an inquiry into this term 'at large' – an analysis, say, of the traditional, that is to say, textbook use of it as compared with more modernist interpretations if, indeed, such latter interpretations existed – he parked this for now, alongside an inquiry into the conditions for ignoring the 'Press Once' instruction printed pleasingly in red around the button that he had so recently pressed twice, focused, as he was, on the situation that he had so cunningly engineered by the very act of pressing the button twice.

Despite the new paragraph in his mind he continued trying to formulate an answer to the questions that he had set himself a little while earlier. His hand moved towards the handrail that ran diagonally or thereabouts down the right-hand side of the stairs as he reflected that he had now expressed to his satisfaction the relationship between the position of the conductress on the stairs, a position of just having crossed the mid-way point or more accurately perhaps, the middle of her torso having just moved from the space occupied by the top deck to the space occupied by the bottom deck, and the timing of his double-pressing of the button at the back of the top deck of the bus. He had, then, explained this juxtaposition to his satisfaction but there remained, to his mind, a pending description of the reasons that he instinctively judged this to be the moment to double-press, or more accurately, that he instinctively judged that the stillness at the mid-point of the double-pressing of the button should correspond to the moment at which the mid-point of the torso of the conductress passed the plane demarcating the lower from the upper deck of the bus. He now attempted to formulate this description. In short, he hoped that the conductress, in being part way down the stairs, would not be able to actually see Marguerite executing the double-press, and, further, would not even be able to tell whether the double-press had taken place on the top or bottom deck of the bus. Granted, that in being aware of Marguerite, with his unkempt appearance, having allowed her to pass before him down the stairs, that the conductress might *suspect* that it was Marguerite who had undertaken the double-press and that, given the circumstances, he had undertaken it on the top deck. Part of his judgement in waiting for her to pass the stair half-way point was that despite this potential suspicion she would, for simplicity's sake, continue to descend, her main concern being the safety of passengers, whether on the bus, having just alighted or attempting to board the bus, a bus, note, that was now moving again. He judged, in short, that she would want to assist confused and possibly injured passengers on the lower deck or in its vicinity before launching an impromptu inquiry, perhaps by asking other passengers where the double-press had taken place and who had been responsible for it. His hand gripped the cool handrail, now, and he reflected that he'd had no intention to cause injury or death in acting as he had. All that he had wanted to do was: a) cause confusion; b) cause the bus to resume its journey, and c) ensure that the stairwell would most likely be clear for his descent, hence the pause which, note, had occurred between chapters, and Marguerite wondered whether this meant that his mind had been entirely blank for the duration of the pause or that there had been nothing of interest occurring in his mind and, if the latter, who judged what was of interest and whether it was a team or an individual who was responsible for this judgement. It was with these thoughts that he came to the end of the chapter, wondering what, if anything, might occur between this ending and the commencement of the next chapter.

38

Marguerite moved his left leg downstairs. More accurately and elegantly, perhaps, he moved his left foot down from the top of the stairs, past the first step down, a step moreover upon which his right foot was resting; he brought, in short, his left foot to rest, momentarily, on the second step down. That was the clearest expression that he could find in his mind at that moment for the act that he was currently engaged in, namely, walking down the curved flight of stairs at the rear of the bus.

He judged that his description of how he was walking down the stairs had advantages and disadvantages. That didn't seem to really capture the action, for him, was one of the disadvantages. One reason he felt it didn't really capture the action was that it failed to bring in the more or less subtle movements of body and mind associated with, or inherent in, the act of swiftly moving a foot, to continue to use that means of describing it, down the stairs, to ensure that he could alight from the bus before it had attained a speed that would be too excessive to be safe for him to alight, this balanced by his wish to have put enough distance between himself and the trailing bus which contained, or had contained, the agents who were trying to apprehend him, as far as he could judge. So much for just one of the disadvantages.

The advantages to his chosen expression included a clear conveyance of the precariousness and the inherent daring and danger associated with the act of moving his left foot down two steps at once: the chosen description conveyed something of the risk involved in what was an instinctive action undertaken at great (or at least at a good) height on an accelerating vehicle in a situation where a slip could have greater than usual consequences – that is, as well as causing himself bodily injury, potentially, if he were to slip, he might also lay himself open to being apprehended by Isobel Absalon and his other pursuers. In describing his movements, then, from the left foot's point of view, as it were, he had emphasised – perhaps overemphasised – the great distance travelled, the constrained space for the reception of that foot at the other end of the process – relative to the size of the foot in question – and the concomitant danger involved in the manoeuvre he was currently engaged in.

Focusing on the toes of the left foot might explicate the point even further. In moving the left foot from the top step to the second step down he was, in a sense, moving the toes of his left foot, which were his final point of contact with the top deck, from the top deck, through the air just above it and then through the air below it, downwards and through a great distance relative to the size of the toes, regardless of whether one chose the big, an intermediate, or the little toe as the yardstick as it were, to land on a constrained area known as the second step down. In focusing more and more on smaller and smaller parts of his anatomy – those parts, such as left leg, left foot and toes of the left foot, note, at the forefront of the action of moving to the second step down, rather than other parts more often at the forefront of his considerations, especially latterly – he was meaning to convey the danger inherent in this act of walking down the stairs.

He hoped it was clear that what he was saying was not inaccurate – the toes on his left foot *had* taken off, so to speak, from the top deck and were about to land, he hoped safely, on the second step down. He could perhaps be accused of not telling the whole truth, but he would vigorously deny this on the basis that he hadn't finished his discourse in this area, m'lud, so how can this accusation be brought against him? Granted that hitherto he had chosen to emphasise smaller and smaller parts of the lower left side of his anatomy (excluding, note, his left testicle) in order to emphasise the precariousness of his swift flight down the stairs, primarily; but who was to say that he wasn't about to bring in the firm foundation provided by his right foot established securely as it was on the first step down and his right hand gripping the diagonal (or thereabouts) handrail running down the right-hand side of the stairwell, a wider perspective that shifted the emphasis to the safety measures that he had implemented to try to ensure his safe passage down the stairs? (No mention, note, of the right testicle, either.) Who could say with certainty that he wasn't about to allude to the rest of his body, that is to say, to the fine balance that he had adopted, instinctively, using his extremities, that is both arms and legs, that is both arms and both legs, in such situations, to ensure, to the best of his ability, that he didn't topple over and fall down the stairs? He had been coming to that, but had intuitively judged that a narrower and narrower focus on smaller and smaller left-side areas of his anatomy (excluding his you-know-what) would best convey the heightened tension that he felt in executing the aforementioned action of moving from the top step to the second step down, stepping over, note, the first step down which, remember, was partially occupied by his right foot, a stepping over that was indicative of his haste in moving down the stairs and of his somewhat reckless attitude to alighting from the bus, an attitude balanced, remember, by the right side of his body which grounded him, as best it could, in the ways described, which is not to say that the different halves of his body or his mind were acting independently of each other. It wasn't to say that at all.

39

With the next step that he took – that of his right foot leaving the first step down to land safely on the third step down, his left foot and right hand providing the safety measures that had, a moment earlier, been provided by his *right* foot and his right hand – his ability to look through the rear window of the top deck of the bus was removed. That is to say that his viewing apparatus, in the specific sense of his eyes, was, or were, below a level, having descended with the rest of his body, whereby he could use it, or them, to look through the window at the rear of the top deck of the bus upon which he was travelling. The position that he now found himself in had both positive and negative implications for his investigation, which he would come onto. But what, firstly, did he really mean when he said that, in moving to the third step down, he could no longer view the scene through the window at the rear of the top deck of the bus? Would the withdrawal of the aforementioned vista have been so sudden, he now wondered? Surely if he craned his neck, as it is known, he would still be able to look through the window at the rear of the top deck of the bus, which continued steadily to accelerate away from the bus stop that it had previously stopped at. He conceded that what he had meant to say was that he could no longer see a useful scene through that window. In other words he thought that, in moving to the third step down, in the sense defined, the view through the rear window of the top deck of the bus upon which he was travelling – the view afforded to him by craning his neck, as it is known – was not one that would provide useful information to him in his investigation into the disappearance of Harold Absalon, the Mayor's transport advisor. He craned his neck in the way described to check whether his assertions in this area were well grounded. He confirmed that they were: all he could see through that window were the mid- and higher-level storeys of the buildings and the tops of trees lining the avenue along which they were travelling, collectively, on that bus. Now this was not to say that those mid- and higher level storeys and tops of trees would not, under different circumstances, be of interest to Marguerite in the course of his inquiries. If, for instance, he suspected that there was a chance that a sniper might be involved in trying to thwart permanently, as it were, his attempts to unearth the circumstances surrounding the disappearance of Harold Absalon and, further, that there was a possibility that the sniper in question, knowing that Marguerite would be travelling on this or another bus along that avenue at around that time and on the day that he was travelling along that avenue and, even further, that the sniper had decided that a good spot to choose for his sniping activities was in the mid- (etc) storeys of a building in the vicinity of the bus stop that the bus upon which Marguerite was travelling had so recently stopped at, given that the bus would most probably be stationary or near-stationary in this vicinity such that, at the sniping moment, to express it in those terms, the sniper would, potentially, have a clear sight of Marguerite, enabling him to take a pot shot at him, as it was known, thereby permanently thwarting, the sniper hoped, Marguerite's investigation into the disappearance of Harold Absalon, the Mayor's transport advisor – then, in that situation, Marguerite would be very interested, of course, in the mid- (etc) storeys. But he had no reason to suspect that a sniper was involved in the disappearance of Harold Absalon; nor did he suspect that a sniper might be involved in trying to thwart permanently him; it was for this reason, amongst others that he would not go into, that he had contended that the view afforded by craning his neck to look through the window at the rear of the top deck of the bus upon which he and others were travelling was not useful in relation to his investigation into the disappearance of the Mayor's transport advisor, which was not to say that the constantly changing view afforded by craning his neck in the way described might not be useful for other reasons, such as bird-watching, to bring in the tree tops which were referred to earlier but had not been considered as even potentially useful by Marguerite in relation to his investigation into Harold Absalon's disappearance. In short, then, it was this combination of having to crane his neck (increasingly uncomfortably as the actual craning continued) to secure a view through the window at the rear of the top deck of the bus, and the fact that the view afforded was of no use to him in his investigation, that he had used the shorthand 'he could no longer see through the window at the rear of the top deck of the bus' – and on reflection, it would have been more accurate to have referred to this window as the window right at the rear of the top deck of the bus upon which he was travelling, given that there were other windows at the rear of that bus, windows on the sides of the bus, that is, and he wouldn't want to confuse the presence of those windows with the window to which he had been referring in his mind throughout this disquisition, namely, the rearmost window on the top deck of the bus upon which he continued to travel.

Nor would he want to confuse different uses of the term 'craning'. The craning involved in craning one's neck was quite different to the craning involved, say, on a construction site, leaving aside any craning of necks on the part of the construction workforce on that site. Marguerite wished, in particular, to make a distinction, in the latter case, between the function of height provision by mechanical crane and the acquisition of height through the craning of one's neck; and the distinction that he wished to make between these two forms was that when one cranes one's neck, as it is known, this was not to say that one's neck became extended in any significant way. A mechanical crane may lift a weight many metres into the air, and this was the paradigm use of the crane, as it were, to Marguerite's mind; similarly, in craning one's neck, one lifted one's head, which can be taken to be the lifted weight in this instance, but the vertical distance traversed by the head through this action of craning one's neck was much, much smaller; this was the only point that Marguerite really wanted to make with regard to craning one's neck. Thus, to illustrate the point further, in craning *his* neck to look out of the rearmost window on the top deck of the bus, as he continued to do whilst continuing to move downstairs, this did not mean that his neck had somehow extended such that his head was now at the level of that window. Sure, in craning one's neck, that neck would extend slightly, having perhaps until the moment of craning been sunken somewhat between one's shoulders. But the extent of the extension of an actual crane, proportionally speaking, would be far in excess of this neck extension however measured, and it is these two senses that Marguerite was wishing to distinguish between, to ensure that they were not confused.

As he continued to descend, he moved his head from an upward- to a downward-looking pose; that is to say that he stopped craning his neck to look out of the rearmost window on the top deck of the bus upon which he was travelling in his pursuit of the circumstances surrounding the disappearance of Harold Absalon knowing, as before, that this craning to look through that window was of absolutely no use to his investigation, for the reasons previously alluded to.

It was only then that he set out the long-promised positive and negative implications for his investigation of the situation he now found himself in: in not being able to look through *either* of the rearmost windows of the bus – that is the rearmost windows on both the upper and lower decks – he was at a disadvantage in not being able to see his pursuers on the bus behind, which was a concern to him; equally he speculated that they would not be able to see him. This situation would not last for long, he realised: his pursuers would very shortly be able to see his legs as they appeared ahead of the top half of his body in the rearmost window on the lower deck of the bus. How was he to ensure the safety of that half of the body given that any damage to that half would affect his body as a whole? It was to this that he would now, perhaps, turn his attention.

40

Having thought, following his intervention with the button at the top of the stairs, that the bus that he was travelling upon would continue to accelerate such that it would carry him sufficiently far from his pursuers on the trailing bus to enable him to shake them off, as it was known, Marguerite was pained to notice that the bus that he was travelling upon had, in fact, already started to decelerate. How could his fine investigative mind have been duped so swiftly, he wondered, as he continued his still unobserved descent at the rear of the bus? Of course, he was in no position to apprehend the cause(s) of the deceleration: just as he could not now see through either of the rearmost windows of the bus that he was travelling upon, nor, by extension, could he see through the foremost windows, that is, the windows right at the front of the top and bottom decks of the bus upon which he was travelling. Given that it was through these foremost windows that he was most likely to apprehend the cause(s) of the deceleration, he was in no real position, literally or metaphorically, to apprehend that cause or those causes. There was a chance, however, that the cause of the deceleration was internal rather than external to the bus. The conductress or one of the passengers on that bus may have found a way of communicating with the driver, indicating, somehow, that the double-press of the button had occurred illegitimately, as it were, and that he should slow down as a precursor to stopping the bus. Still other, more plausible, internal causes could be conceived of, including the commonplace one of the momentary deceleration of the bus as the driver changed gear, as it was known. Marguerite felt reasonably sure, if this latter case pertained, that the bus would start to accelerate again following the gear change – that had been his experience on numerous occasions whilst travelling in motorised and other road vehicles in broadly similar circumstances in the past. But he could not be sure, until that re-acceleration took place, that this was the situation as it pertained to him at that moment – that is, a situation in which he was travelling in a vehicle that was in the process of ascending, numerically speaking, through the gears, or at least ascending, numerically speaking, from one gear to the next, the former, in this case, likely to be the first and the latter being the second gear – and it was for this reason that he could not rule out the other cause(s), whether internal or external to the bus, for the unexpected deceleration of the bus.

He found himself trying to find firm expositional ground just as his foot (unspecified) was travelling towards the fourth step down, a manoeuvre, moreover, that had become more precarious given that the bus had suddenly started decelerating following a period of acceleration that Marguerite had asserted would continue if not indefinitely then at least until he had shaken off his pursuers on the trailing bus. The reason he sought firmer ground for his rhetorical flourishes, rhetorical, note, only in a sotto voce sense, was that he had seen the ground beneath his assertion of continued and sufficient acceleration fall away so quickly and so easily. This had shaken his confidence, in short. He expressed this new unsteadiness externally by taking hold, now, of both handrails, that is, by gripping, on both sides of the stairwell, the rails that had been provided by the bus company for the purpose of steadying one's body (and, by extension, one's mind, Marguerite contended) at moments when the speed of the bus or the rate of its acceleration or deceleration changed abruptly or when the bus abruptly moved from a state of acceleration to one of deceleration, as in the current instance, or vice versa, or even to a state of abrupt braking. How could he trust his own assertions now, he wondered, when they so swiftly fell apart in the face of the evidence?

Just at that moment the driver moved into what Marguerite was sure was second gear and the bus started to accelerate again. With this, Marguerite regained his investigative composure. He explained now, that what he had meant to assert, previously, was that the bus would follow a broadly accelerative *trend* for the duration of his descent to its lower deck and that the sweep of this accelerative trend, as it were, would be sufficient to carry him far enough away from his pursuers on the trailing bus to enable him to shake them off, as it is known. The broadly accelerative trend did not, of course, rule out moments of deceleration such as the one that he had so recently experienced, provided that such moments were a small proportion of that trend. Having regained his mental footing in this way he regained his actual, that is to say his physical footing by placing his foot – the left, note – on the fourth step down. He further exhibited his regained composure, confidence – flamboyance, even – by removing one hand – the left – from the handrail running down the left hand side of the stairwell, meaning that he was now only holding onto one handrail – the one to his right – and by offering the following additional assertions: that the transition from second to third gear was still some moments away; that, despite the remaining four steps, the bus would still be travelling slowly enough for him to disembark, when the time came, without causing undue injury to himself; and, finally, that he was firmly back on the trail of Harold Absalon, the Mayor's transport advisor, who, remember, was still missing[v].

v. Perhaps unsurprisingly, given the number of night-shifts I was putting in analysing tapes of Isobel Absalon's movements, my performance in my day job declined. This saddened me – I'd been given such an opportunity following his disappearance, but it was as if the investigative task he'd left me was designed such that, ultimately, I would never step into his shoes, as it were. This, then, was his bequest to me: a precious opportunity that was continually just beyond my grasp.

41

Immediately he spotted an anomaly: most of the fingers of his right hand were located to the right of the right-hand handrail, as that right hand slid down that right-hand handrail in steadying his descent. In what sense, then, was that handrail to his right, as he had so recently asserted? Would it have been better, he now wondered, to have asserted that the right-hand handrail was *mostly* to his right whilst noting that most of his right hand was, in fact to the right of that right-hand handrail? He would leave that for others to decide, he decided. But before leaving this point entirely, he felt the need to clarify the term 'most'.

Marguerite wished to clarify that he was using the term 'most' in an analogue rather than a digital sense, with the term digital relating, he thought, in the situation under consideration, to whole fingers or persons, whereas analogue related, in the same situation, to parts of fingers or persons. Thus when Marguerite had asserted that most of the fingers of his right hand were to the right of the right-hand handrail, and that he meant this in an analogue rather than a digital sense, he was holding that, proportionately rather than numerically, most of the fingers of his right hand were to the right of the right-hand handrail whilst most of his person was to the left of the right-hand handrail. It was not, then, that, say, the middle, ring and little finger of his right hand, in their entirety, were to the right of the handrail previously referred to whilst his right forefinger, to use that shorthand, was to the left of that handrail, leaving aside, for the time being, the question of whether the thumb counted as a finger or necessitated its own category. If he had been using the term 'most' in the digital sense partially explained above coupled, so to speak, with the position that thumbs should occupy their own category separate from that which fingers occupy, as it were, then, in asserting that most of his fingers were to the right of the right-hand handrail, what he would have been saying, given that he had a full complement of fingers on his right hand, which is to say that his right hand incorpo-rated a total of four fingers and a thumb (not that he was deficient in that department in relation to his left hand), was that his right forefinger (etc), in its entirety, was to the left of the handrail (as before) alongside his thumb (which was an innocent party in this inquiry for what he hoped were now obvious reasons) whilst his right middle-, ring- and little fingers, in their entirety, were to the right of that handrail. Such was an example of the sums, if one took the thumb to fall outside the category of 'finger'. Anatomi-cally speaking this was a perfectly acceptable position for the hand to adopt in the case of the majority of subjects, and if it were to adopt such a position it would be accurate to say that most of the fingers of Marguerite's right hand were to the right of the right-hand handrail in the digital sense expounded earlier. Another example in which, arguably, most of the fingers of Marguerite's right hand would be to the right of the right-hand handrail in the digital sense was the situation in which all of the fingers of Marguerite's right hand were to the right of the right-hand hand rail, an example that more closely approximated to the situation on the ground, as it were. But for Marguerite to assert that either of these examples was the case in the current situation would be for him to fabricate evidence, or, in the latter case, to not tell the whole truth, something that, given his professionalism and integrity, he would not countenance. His hand was not strictly speaking in either of the digital positions described; that is, digitally speaking, the majority of the fingers of his right hand were not to the right of the right-hand handrail, given that they re-emerged underneath and then to the left of that handrail; nor, then, could it be asserted that all of his fingers were in that position, unless one considered that the parts of those fingers that were to the left of the right-hand handrail were just so much irrelevant 'noise' from a digital viewpoint, and Marguerite was not willing to do this, for some reason. That was why, as he placed his right foot onto the fifth step down, noticing, for the first time, that there was someone with blonde hair to the *right* of that handrail, seemingly waiting for him in what could be called the conductor's position beside the stairway as it extended part-way across the open platform on the lower deck, he had explicitly noted that it was in an analogue rather than a digital sense that most of the fingers of his right hand were (or should that be 'was'?) to the right of the right-hand handrail whilst most of his person was to the left of that handrail. He completed his dissertation on the digital and analogue in relation to one's digits, whilst trying to ascertain the gender of the person waiting for him by seeing if he could look, from his vantage point, down the front of their top, with the succinct note that whilst the same applies to one's toes, the specific situation in relation to hand- (or in that case foot-) rails was unlikely to arise unless, as in the case of cliff-hangers, one is a chimpanzee or other of the so-called lower apes.

42

Marguerite heard music, as his left foot approached the sixth step down, also known as the second step up, in his on-going movement towards the lower deck of the bus. In fact he realised that he'd been hearing music for some little while, but it was only now that it fully entered his – and for that reason, our – consciousness. At the same time a pair of shapely female legs appeared within his field of vision from the right, enabling him to take his eyes from what he had taken to be the freckled tops of Isobel Absalon's lovely breasts[w], almost directly below him. He could not prevent himself from putting the two new pieces of evidence together: he wondered, given the music, whether the legs, which were approaching his projected landing point at the bottom of the stairs, belonged to a person known as a busker.

Buskers were people who played music or engaged in other performances publicly with a view to being paid for those performances by other passengers, in the case of those buskers travelling on public transport, or by passers-by, in the case of those buskers who were not on any

w. What I found in the nightly footage was increasingly shocking to me, to the extent that I thought that I must be losing my mind.

form of transport, at least not any moving form of transport. This situation was different, note, to the scenario in which someone was just whistling to themselves or listening to a personal or other sort of stereo, say, however loudly, regardless of whether the person engaged in those private acts defined themselves, under somewhat different circumstances, as a busker. That was to say that there was more to the musical busker than music publicly expressed. The busker had to want to busk at that moment and must be open to the possibility that those hearing their music would want to give money to them for hearing that music; in fact, the busker would actively encourage the giving of money by making available, for example, a hat or other headpiece proffered in an inverse position to that employed when actually wearing the hat or other headpiece, with this proffering occurring either in the hand of the busker, a hand, that is, holding the hat (etc) in the direction of the person or people from whom he or she expected to receive funds, or through placing the hat (etc) in that inverse position on the ground between themselves and their potential donors. This latter means of proffering the hat was not generally used by buskers busking on public transport. The reason for this was that the busker in question would, despite the fact that they were already travelling via the propulsion of the public transport vehicle in question, have to walk around within that vehicle in order to collect funds, perhaps even moving from that vehicle to the next, where those vehicles were coupled, as it were, to each other, as in the case of train carriages, whether on an under- or overground railway, whereas in the case of the busker busking on the pavement or sidewalk, say, they wouldn't necessarily need to move towards their potential funders in this way, the assumption being, Marguerite thought, that the potential funders in this scenario would move towards *them*: they would, for example, be walking past the busker in this case, especially if the busker had chosen their position carefully, that is, provided that the busker had chosen a position that was a busy pedestrian thoroughfare and one in which the pedestrians: a) could not easily avoid hearing the music that the busker was performing with a view to receiving money for this performance and b) could not easily avoid walking past the inverted hat placed on the ground for the purpose of receiving the funds alluded to in a) above.

Non-buskers requesting funds whilst travelling on public transport were a different category entirely, at least in relation to the means of fund-collection: this latter group did not tend to use the upturned hat or other head-piece as a means of securing such funds; much more often, in Marguerite's experience, they used a bare or, granted, partially clad hand (the latter in the case of the finger-less glove) outstretched in the direction of the potential funder. Alternatively a dirty, rim-chewed polystyrene cup proffered in a similar fashion to the busker's inverted hat would be employed, although note, here, that the cup, in this case, could not be taken to be in an inverted position for what Marguerite hoped were obvious reasons.

The reason for the existence of this difference between the busker and the majority, at least, of beggars, as that portion of the non-busking, street- or public transport-based fundraising population was known, was to do with the different styles employed by these different groups. Musicians, in summary, tended to wear hats not just for the purpose of garnering funds but because hats were often associated with a sense of style that adhered to the ideal of musicianship, at least in the 'popular' and especially in the 'jazz' genre. The hat, in short, was an effervescence, as it were, of the natural sense of style often associated with musicians. A different sense of style was generally associated with the non-busking vagrant, one that, whilst it didn't rule out the donning or, indeed, doffing of a hat, was not naturally associated with that group of individuals in the way it was with musicians in the popular, jazz, blues and some other genres. Therein, quite simply, lay the difference, to Marguerite's mind.

Two further pieces of evidence offered themselves to him, as his left foot attained the sixth step down the stairway at the rear of the bus upon which he was travelling: firstly, that the top of the legs in question was covered in blue pinstriped cloth in the form of a short skirt and, secondly, that the music was coming from what is known as a ghetto blaster held in the lap of someone sitting in the seat diagonally across the platform from his projected landing point at the base of the stairs. This expansion to his evidence base enabled him to disassociate the delightful legs in question, which had now stopped moving towards him, from the music, as it were: he concluded that they belonged, in fact, to the woman in the pinstriped suit who was, once again, helping him. She was helping him in this case by blocking the exit from the main part of the lower deck to the platform at the rear of the bus. And the reason that she was doing this, Marguerite surmised, was to prevent the conductress from apprehending him, thereby leaving him at liberty to continue his investigation into the disappearance of Harold Absalon, the Mayor's transport advisor, provided, of course, that he could find a way of slipping past the scintillating Isobel Absalon[x] at the base of the stairs.

x. Night after night, as I rewound and replayed the tapes, I found her going to bed, generally between 2200 and 2230 hours and, not long after, a male figure slipping into bed beside her.

43

Marguerite realised, as his right foot approached the seventh step down the curved stairwell at the rear of the bus, that this step represented both the final step and, in a different sense, the penultimate step. What he meant by this, he thought, was, quite simply, that the step that he, in the form, in particular, of his right foot, was approaching was, when taking a top-down approach, as it were, the final step in that stairwell, in that he would come across no more of these three-dimensional right angles, if one can call them that, in his descent of that particular stairwell on that occasion. Once, in other words, his foot – the right – had attained this step, there would be no more of these vertiginous elevatory devices to be encountered. At the same time, however, there would, of course, still be a step for him to take in reaching the open platform at the rear of the bus upon which he was travelling, and this step could, quite reasonably and uncontroversially, *also* be called the final step. It was in this sense, then, that he had maintained, as his right foot had commenced its approach to the seventh step down, that the impending step represented both the final step and, in a different sense, the penultimate step. It depended, in essence, on one's viewpoint: from the stairwell's point of view, as it were, this seventh step down was the final step that it had to offer the person descending; however, the person descending still had to take this step, as it was known, and, in so doing, make a step, somehow. To take Marguerite's own situation, once again, as an example: the action of his right foot, in moving from the fifth, past his left foot on the sixth, to the seventh step down resulted in him both attaining the final step in that stairwell whilst still, somehow, having to make that final step. Given, then, that there remained a step to be made once he had attained the final step in that stairwell, Marguerite was maintaining that the step that had resulted, or would result, in his attainment of this final step was, in fact, but in a somewhat different sense, the penultimate step. How, after all, could it be the final step when there was one step still left to be taken? And if this was because this final step was somehow to be made then why couldn't one continue making these so-called final steps indefinitely, making, in the process, a nonsense of the whole concept of finality in relation, at least, to steps?

He realised, as his right foot continued to approach the seventh step down the stairwell at the rear of the bus upon which he was travelling, that he would have to take a step back – not literally – in this branch of his inquiry in an attempt to make it sufficiently clear for him to proceed with the main part of his investigation. The way that he took this metaphorical step backwards was by examining, more closely, the terms that he had been using in his approach to the assertion that the final step also somehow represented the penultimate step in that stairwell. He was keen to examine, in particular, how it was, when one had attained what was, from the stairwell's point of view, as it were, the final step, that this step still remained to be taken or made. In what sense, in short, could one take something that one already had? Equally, or thereabouts, how could one make something that one had already attained? If, more specifically, one had attained the final step whilst still having to take it, then where, exactly, did one stand? It was, at first sight, deeply perplexing to Marguerite.

One area that he thought worthy of further investigation as a means of helping him to get out of the tight spot that he now found himself in, as he approached the final or the penultimate step, depending on one's viewpoint, related to what he thought of as consumables; in particular he wondered, as his foot continued its mid-stair flight, whether a comparison between stepping and eating might prove fruitful. Could it be said that one attained a step in the same way that one attained, say, a candy bar; just as in the case of the candy bar, the attainment of the step and its consumption, as it were, were quite different things. One attained it and then one ate it, in the case of the candy bar; in the case of the step, one attained it and then one ate it *up*, perhaps. A classical usage came into Marguerite's mind at that moment: that of eating up the ground, in his case, between himself and Harold Absalon; he was satisfied, partially, with that.

A further, potentially helpful analogy yielded itself to Marguerite's mind at that moment: that of sexual conquest. Perhaps, in a similar way to the candy bar, one attained a mate, in the sexual sense, and then one had them, again, in the sexual sense. In that instance, the attainment and the possession were, again, quite different things; one got someone and then one took them, as it were, even if that person belonged to someone else[y], so to speak. Again, Marguerite felt partially satisfied with this and felt, further, that it was taking him closer, once again, to the circumstances surrounding the disappearance of Harold Absalon, the Mayor's transport advisor.

But in what sense could one *make* something that one already had? More specifically, how, once one had attained the final step could one *make* it? If that or any other step was akin to the consumable then how could one, in the very same act, both consume and somehow fabricate it? Equally, approximately, in the arena of sexual conquest, how could one both have and make one's mate? Granted, in the case of the female conquest of the male it could be said, in Marguerite's experience, that 'she made him into the man he is today'; this 'made man', as he would, perhaps, be referred to, may well have been made, in large part, so to speak, through the act of sexual conquest, in which case the having and the making could, perhaps, be taken to be coterminous. But the reverse position, so to speak, could not be held, to Marguerite's mind: that of the man having the woman, as was much more usual to his mind, whilst also somehow making her. It just made no sense, to his mind.

Perhaps nobody actually, in practice, referred to making a step, aside, of course, from the actual physical construc-

---

[y]. Nothing so funny about that, you might think. After all, Harold must have suspected that she was up to something, otherwise he wouldn't have put me on her tail.

tion of such items in a factory. Perhaps he had simply confused the making of with the taking of a step because of the rhyme. Even if this were the case, meaning that he could be wholly rather than just partially satisfied with the analogy between steps and consumables, on the one hand, and between steps and sexual conquest, on the other (and in rare, delicious cases, both hands at once, as it were), it would, he now realised, as his right foot came even closer to actually attaining the seventh step down, still leave him with a difficulty. Even when, to return once again to Marguerite's case, one attained the final step and one started to take that step, *still another step would remain* after one had touched down on the lower deck – this final final step, as it were, being, in Marguerite's situation, that of the right foot moving from the final step to join the left foot on the lower deck. In other words, his right foot would attain the seventh step down, which was the final step from the stairwell's point of view; his left would then take off, as it were, from the sixth step down, en route to the lower deck itself, and this step was one that could be taken, also, to represent the final step; finally, his right foot would leave the seventh step down, the final step from the stairwell's point of view, as before, to commence its journey towards the left foot which was, remember, resting, momentarily, on the lower deck, having made what Marguerite had hitherto taken to be the final step and, in making this journey, would make what Marguerite now referred to as the final final step but which he could, he now realised, choose, for what he hoped were now obvious reasons, to refer to as the final final final step.

He had hoped, through the foregoing, to have shown to his subordinates, and others following his investigation through whatever mysterious means, that one could not make indefinite final steps when descending a staircase at the rear of a bus. That he had failed in this task shook his confidence somewhat, as his right foot failed, in fact, to land on the seventh step down but instead proceeded directly towards the lower deck in what could surely, now, be taken to represent the final or penultimate step down the stairwell of the bus upon which he was travelling in pursuit of Harold Absalon, the Mayor's transport advisor, who was missing.

44

Why, Marguerite wondered, as he saw something ahead of him that represented a major leap forwards in his investigation, had he chosen, suddenly, to take two steps at once, as it is known, in his descent of the stairwell at the rear of the bus upon which he was travelling, such that his right foot was now directly approaching the lower deck rather than the stairwell's final step? The answer to that question was, for once, quite straightforward, he thought, as he took in more of the scene beyond the open platform in front of him in an attempt to confirm what he had seen: he had realised that he needed, quite simply, to stay one step ahead of Isobel Absalon, who was still waiting for him at the foot of the stairs in the position where the conductor would often ordinarily stand. Rather, he had realised, suddenly, that he needed to stay *at least* one step ahead of Isobel Absalon, whose perfumed presence he could sense just behind his right shoulder, or thereabouts; by feigning to attain the stairwell's final step and then, during his right foot's final approach towards that step, suddenly applying thrust, as it were, he was able to re-elevate his foot such that it was able to clear that step and move directly for the lower deck of the bus upon which it – and he – was travelling, thereby enabling him to stay that necessary minimum number of steps ahead of Isobel Absalon. Not that he wanted to stay one step ahead of Isobel Absalon, as a minimum; he wanted, in fact, for the minimum distance between them to be much less than one step and, furthermore, for them to be facing each other at the moment of nearest approach, as it were; however, for reasons of professional etiquette and procedure he felt unable to bring this about at that moment, focused, as he remained, on the pursuit of her husband, Harold Absalon, the Mayor's transport advisor, who was still missing. He could not, of course, rule out the possibility of Isobel Absalon responding to his attempt to stay at least one step ahead of her by extending her stride to gain on him once again[z]; the thought of this thrilled Marguerite, but he did not dwell upon it, knowing that he needed to turn his mind, finally, to the decisive scene that had opened up in front of him just a few moments before, to bring some sort of satisfaction to his numerous followers, at least. It had only been a moment, but he was certain, in short, that he had actually seen Harold Absalon, the Mayor's transport advisor, in one of the showrooms lining the avenue along which the bus was travelling. Not only did this confirm that Harold Absalon was still, in fact, alive, of course, it also confirmed to Marguerite that he had, indeed, been on the trail of Harold Absalon all along.

The bus continued to accelerate, his left foot joined his right on the lower deck, and he moved swiftly, now, across the platform, with its lines of ridges, which he assumed, in

z. No, it wasn't the regularity of her indecency that disturbed me; it was the fact that the figure I witnessed getting into that king-sized bed night after night, and doing all those unspeakable things to her was *me*.

passing, were there to help passengers keep their footing in that area. Approaching the edge of the platform, he looked back in the direction in which he had seen Harold Absalon. The window of the showroom in question now just reflected the trailing bus, which was, once again, gaining on them, on the inside, and travelling at quite a speed. Without looking behind him – without, in short, a further thought for Isobel Absalon – he stepped off the platform.

ACKNOWLEDGEMENTS

I would like to thank Samaggavasans past and present for the supportive conditions in which to write this book, and for listening to and commenting upon various drafts over the years. In particular I'd like to thank Parama-bandhu, Jnanavaca, Maitreyaraja, Stephen Heppell, Aaron Matheson, Rob Hirsch, Phap Dan, Geoff Sheridan, Mattias Herbertson, Canute Clarke, Knut Wilmott, Jed Shamel, Anthony Wright, Adam Berrisford, Jim Taylor, but most of all Maitreyabandhu without whose friendship, interest, belief and guidance I doubt the book would have been written. Thanks, also, to mum and David, Sanghasiha, Kyle Brown, David O'Neill, Victoria Okotie, Tony and Anne Okotie, Maitripushpa, Linda Mannheim, Izabella Grogan, Kalyanavaca, Vidyadaka, David John and Paul Gapper for interest, help and faith over the years. Thank you to Karen Hart, publicity person extraordinaire, and such fun to work with, and to Simon Hardeman. Thanks, also, to John Oakey for the beautiful cover, to David Rose and Lee Rourke, for comments on advance copies, and to *The White Review*, for publishing early chapters. I feel hugely fortunate to have an editor of the calibre of Nicholas Royle, and it is a privilege to have such exciting and enthusiastic publishers as Jen and Chris Hamilton-Emery. And to my darling SuYen Tan, for your kindness and perseverance in spending significant time with one whose mind can get caught in such self-regarding ruminations as contained herein: heartfelt thanks, and love.